DIRT

Denise Gosliner Orenstein

For André Bertram Siegel

and for Duncan and McNeill,
brave, naughty, and magically intuitive pony friends

Library of Congress Cataloging-in-Publication Data

Names: Orenstein, Denise Gosliner, 1950- author.
Title: Dirt / Denise Orenstein.
Description: First edition. | New York, NY : Scholastic Press, 2017. | Summary: Eleven-year-old Yonde
stopped talking when her mother died, and she stopped going to school because of the bullies, knowing
her father would never even notice (although the social worker did); indeed the only creature that seems
care about her is the one-eyed Shetland pony called Dirt who lives on the neighboring farm—so when s
discovers that Dirt is about to be sold for horsemeat she is determined to find a way to save him.
Identifiers: LCCN 2016045585 (print) | LCCN 2017003405 (ebook) | ISBN 9780545925853
(hardcover : alk. paper) | ISBN 9780545925860 (pbk. : alk. paper) | ISBN 9780545925877 (ebook)
Subjects: LCSH: Shetland pony—Juvenile fiction. | Human-animal relationships—Juvenile fiction. | Ani
welfare—Juvenile fiction. | Fathers and daughters—Juvenile fiction. | Dysfunctional families—Juveni
fiction. | Foster home care—Juvenile fiction. | CYAC: Shetland pony—Fiction. | Ponies—Fiction. |
Human-animal relationships—Fiction. | Animals—Treatment—Fiction. |
Fathers and daughters—Fiction. | Family life—Fiction.
Classification: LCC PZ7.O6314 Di 2017 (print) | LCC PZ7.O6314 (ebook) | DDC 813.6 [[Fic]] —dc2
LC record available at https://lccn.loc.gov/2016045585

10 9 8 7 6 5 4 3 2 1   17 18 19 20 21

Printed in the U.S.A.   23
First edition, August 2017

Book design by Nina Goffi
Illustration page 174 by Nina Goffi for Scholastic

To hear, one must be silent.

Ursula K. LeGuin, *A Wizard of Earthsea*

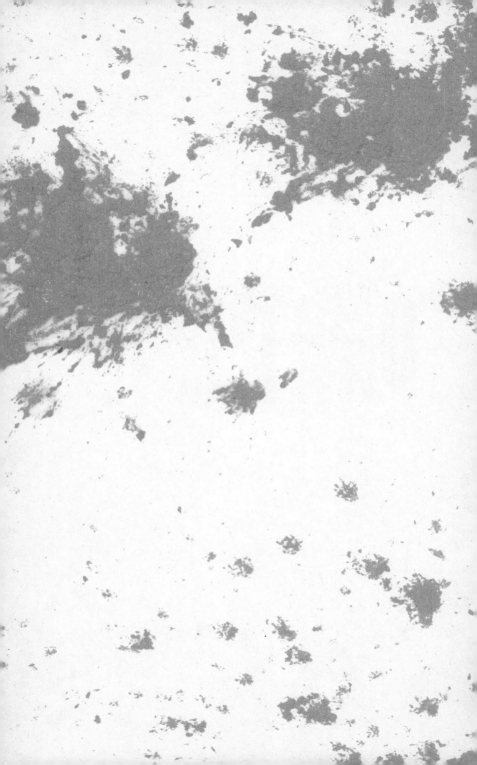

PART ONE

My Rocky Road

My father once explained that they named me Yonder because there's always something to learn, way up ahead, yonder. Always a surprise right around the corner, sometimes sweet and sometimes sad, but always a fork in the road that could change your life.

When my mother died four years ago, my father said, "Here is the fork, Yonder. Here is the learning just up ahead. We can choose to stop moving up that rocky path or we can decide something else. What will you do? What will we do together?"

Silence draped my little crooked house and the windows went dark. I crawled into quiet and decided to stay there. After all, words didn't work. Did it really matter if you called out at night, all alone in your narrow bed: *Bring her back. Please bring my mother back.*

Did it matter if you yelled at the top of your lungs until your throat hurt? If you yelled and yelled for her and there wasn't a single answer?

It did not. It did not matter one bit.

So I decided not to speak. Silence seemed safer.

"An unusual childhood disorder," the clinic doctor told my father, but it was almost as if my father hardly noticed that I stopped speaking. He was so lost in his own sadness.

One afternoon at the Shelter Library, I looked up "speech disorders and children" and found this: "a condition in which a child who can speak stops speaking because of trauma or anxiety." *Well*, I thought, *I suppose the doctor might have gotten it right*, although I wasn't sure if I really could speak anymore, even if I wanted to. I wasn't sure and I was scared to try.

What if I opened my mouth and ugly words spilled out? Better to be quiet than say what it was like to lose my mother and father at the same time, my mother in body and spirit and my father just in spirit. While he hadn't died in the car accident, he was not the same father as before. This new father heaved himself around the house as if his body were filled with cement.

This is what I remember about my mother: how she loved to read to me before I went to sleep at night, the way her cheeks pinked up in the fall, and the broken front tooth that she cracked when we were ice-skating on the Shelter town pond. I remember my mother's short, wavy dark hair and the soft khaki jacket that she wore even inside. The one with the blue ink stain on the left shoulder, both sleeves torn to the elbow, making it look like she had four arms. My mother's fingernails were long and splintered from cold Vermont winters; sometimes they scratched my scalp when she brushed my hair. She smelled like maple syrup, burnt sugar, overripe apple.

Even though I was little, I knew that the fork in the road my father talked about offered only one possibility. We would surely walk that rocky path because we didn't have a choice. We would move forward because there was no going back. The fork in the road was there, just as he always told me, but we would take the more difficult turn and keep struggling uphill. And so we did.

I didn't understand how rocky a road could be back then. I didn't understand how slippery or how full of twists and turns. And then my fork led the way to a lonely pony who needed me as much as I needed him. But I didn't know Dirt was coming way back then.

A Four-Armed Octopus

That fall, school started earlier than usual, something that I found to be irritating, to say the least. The end of August was still summer, wasn't it, and it should have been illegal for school to start before September.

The school hallways still had their musty smell, the lightbulbs in the stairways still flickered on and off, and the kids were already waiting to find someone, anyone who was different. That someone seemed to be me.

On the Friday morning before Labor Day weekend, I stomped briskly up Robert Frost Middle School's concrete steps and through the double front doors, my arms wound around my khaki jacket like a four-armed octopus, determined not to let anyone get my goat. I found it helpful to remember that an octopus has three whole hearts—if one was ever broken, there'd always be another two to fall back on.

In any case, a long weekend was just ahead and nothing was going to get me down.

I tried to start each day at school the same way: shoulders squared, arms wrapped around my chest, my head held high. But, sure enough, it wasn't a few minutes before I heard someone calling behind me. I immediately recognized that nasal, high-pitched voice: It belonged to none other than the one and only disgusting Heywood Prune.

Prune was short and stumpy with a slash of blistery lips, pink rabbit eyes, a shaved head, and pale skin. He smelled like corn chips, and his nail-bitten fingers were stained from the red pistachio nuts that he always kept crammed in his pockets. Not appetizing, to say the least.

I'd known Heywood Prune since kindergarten. Lucky me.

And peculiar that such a shrunken varmint turned out to be the biggest bully of my life. How did that even happen? It wasn't as if I couldn't take care of myself or was easily pushed around. Hardly. I was tough as they come.

Yet Prune somehow knew how to make my life miserable.

"Whatcha doing, Miss Deaf and Dumb?" His words smashed against my back like hard-packed snowballs as I walked down the hall.

I may have dropped my head just a little. I may have picked up my pace just a tad.

Prune chortled. His ugly laugh sounded like a smelly hyena's, although I had never actually heard or seen a hyena in person before. Actually, maybe they weren't smelly at all.

"Who's fonder of Yonder?" Prune's voice was squawking loudly and I heard his steps catch up to mine. The scent of corn chips made me swallow hard. But I kept marching forward. I knew not to stop.

"No one's fonder of Yonder!"

The little creep was on a roll.

"Hey, Yonder," he continued. I imagined a foam of white spit flying from his blistery mouth. "Headed to your locker?"

Actually, I *was* going to my locker. I needed to hang up my jacket and find my language arts composition book. Luckily, my locker was just a few steps away. Unluckily, Prune and a growing gang of followers were right behind me.

I stood still for a second, thinking about a possible escape, but it was too late. The boys crowded together, chortling and licking their lips in anticipation. Maybe some stupid Robert Frost teacher or even Principal Flint would make a surprise appearance to provide emergency assistance. And it wasn't often that I wished for the appearance of any adult at school. No way, no how.

The first thing I saw was that my locker handle was coated with greenish slime. Yuck. But I pretended not to notice. This had happened several times before—someone leaving nose cooties all over the handle—and I didn't want to give Prune and his followers the satisfaction of seeing my horror and disgust all over again. So I simply nudged the locker open with my elbow and reached inside for my book.

I heard the mash of boys behind me squeal. I felt dampness on my hands and looked down. There was something strange about the blue-and-white gym shorts that were hanging on my locker hook and that brushed my arm below. Yes, there was definitely an inky black mark of some kind and a sharp, familiar odor filled my nostrils. It reminded me of the cleaning stuff my father sometimes squirted on our dirty kitchen table when I'd stained it with paint or marker. I squinted in concentration. The smell grew stronger. The boys laughed with pure delight.

"Oh, Yonder"—Prune was practically bent over in glee—"guess you won't be wearing your gym shorts today!" And then Prune and his entire crew pranced gleefully in unison, just like they'd rehearsed their ugly dance in Mr. Tisdale's performing arts mobile (think trailer) classroom. Mr. Tisdale had insisted we all learn the authentic version of the Virginia reel, something I was actually quite good at.

"Yonder can't wear her gym shorts!" the mini-mob chanted mindlessly.

Clearly, these nitwits were one sandwich short of a picnic.

I looked down at my shorts again. What was that smell, and why were the shorts beginning to glob together? And it quickly became apparent that the pretty, faux-silk fabric was attached to my hand. Yup, no doubt about it. The hems of my brand-new gym shorts were covered with glue and pen ink, the very same cement glue and black ink we had used the day before to make our class Greek diorama. All at once, I recognized the odor and I felt the squish on my fingers. The glue was apparently yet to dry and probably never would. Silk and adhesive are not a good mix. It figured that Prune and his band of idiots didn't realize that.

Prune was laughing so hard that I thought he might choke. Then he grabbed my shorts right out of my hand and smashed them back into the right sleeve of my mother's khaki jacket so there was glue everywhere, all over me.

That's when I lost it. I felt my face and neck turn the color of my hair.

I hate all of you, I screamed in my head. *You're a bunch of pathetic losers!*

I spun around to face my enemies, throwing my composition book at Prune and then waving the gym shorts in front of my face like a weapon. Matadors in Spain have been known to use the exact same move in bullfights.

To my surprise and relief, Prune and each and every one of his gang had somehow vanished. There wasn't a single fifth-grade delinquent in sight. Instead, to my surprise and distress, my previous wish from a few moments before came true right in front of my flushed face.

"Young lady," Principal Flint said sharply, hands on her hips, "what in high heavens has gotten into you?"

I craned my neck to look down the corridor, on the look-out for the missing criminals. I wanted to tell her what in high heavens had gotten into me. I wanted to tell her about how miserable Heywood Prune was making my life. But as usual, I had no words.

Principal Flint raised her voice an octave.

"Yonder," she said without an ounce of sympathy, "I'm really mystified about your behavior lately, but enough is enough." She wiped her forehead in what seemed to me to be a very theatrical gesture. "This is the second example of your poor behavior this month. We're still cleaning up those unpleasant things you wrote about your fellow students on your desk. Permanent marker is called that for good reason. My office right now!"

Let me tell you:

Justice is most definitely blind.

Principal Flint suspended me for two days, so I stopped going to stupid Robert Frost Middle School for an entire week. Just like that. Why not? Why shouldn't I live it up and prolong the suspension as long as I liked? Who would even notice or care? Our home phone had been cut off for months, and I hid the first school notice, and then the official school letter, from my father without a second thought. He slept until late afternoon on the days he didn't work anyway, and on work days at the orchard, my father didn't get home until early evening. That's when he made it into work at all.

"How's school, darlin'?" he'd sometimes ask absentmindedly over a dinner of baked apples or apple bread. "Learn anything?"

I'd nod and he'd nod.

Then he'd smile and lay his large paw of a heavy hand next to mine and look right at me, his eyes glassy. Sometimes he'd say gruffly, "Wish I was a better dad to you, my Yonder girl. Wish I could be better."

And soon my eyes would water from the hot apple steam and his eyes would water too and we'd look at each other like strangers. Then I would almost be able to see both of our hearts fill as clearly as a glass pitcher poured with cider. I'd see our two battered hearts fill, the way a sinking car fills up with pond water, the way a grave fills up with earth. A heart so flooded isn't worth squat.

But I was wrong about some things back then, and I was wrong that nobody noticed I stopped going to school.

The Beast
Befriends Me

Skipping school is all that it's cracked up to be. No kidding.
Every child should experience it. I highly recommend playing hooky.

Since Monday was a holiday, my suspension began on
Tuesday, giving me a full three days of official freedom.
These days went by quickly as I spent the mornings happily
digging for coins in my backyard pond. Once I found three
dollars in quarters in that same spot, but that was a whole
year ago when I was ten. This time, I didn't have much luck,
only discovering one nickel and two pennies. This didn't
dampen my spirits one bit, however, and I enjoyed my afternoons of freedom, watching the same frog jump into our
mossy pond, pop up, then dive all over again. Maybe it
wasn't the same exact frog after all.

By Thursday morning, my first day of actual delinquency, I was ready for a real adventure. And adventure is exactly what I found.

It all started with an early fall pumpkin that I had rolled home from the side of the road. It was easy to find pumpkins and squashes in the fall, often pockmarked and oddly shaped, abandoned on the edges of fields. My father said it was a particularly early pumpkin harvest that year, and that many of them wouldn't last until Halloween.

I didn't care. Halloween was a dumb holiday anyway and we had to turn off all of our lights in the little crooked house each year since we never had any candy to give out. And I'd always have to keep an eye out for signs of stupid trickery—it can be exhausting to be on guard all night.

The pumpkin in question was badly bruised and clearly abandoned for some caring individual to take. Without a second thought, I claimed it as my own.

In any case, I was minding my own business, sitting on my front steps, whiling away the afternoon by listening to the trees as they began to lose their first leaves. My rescued pumpkin rested its misshapen back against the top step and I proceeded to poke at it with two fingers. I watched as the orangey-yellowish skin fell open at my touch. The pumpkin smell was sweet and sour at the same time, making me both hungry and somewhat sick to my stomach. Overhead, the clouds went dark, and before I knew what was what, a trickle of warm raindrops turned into a steady beat.

The rain grew stronger and stronger, the wind blowing hard, but I just sat there, enjoying the water streaming down over my head, watching the old pumpkin disintegrate in the heavy storm and feeling my hair swooping all over the place like a big red bird diving for food. Sometimes, a good rainstorm is just what the doctor ordered, and the wetter I got, the happier I felt. After all, the kids at Robert Frost were probably in stuffy math class right then, chewing on their stumpy pencils and trying to cheat off of each other's papers. Who needed that?

Rain poured over my shoulders and my face; when I tried to open my eyes wide, all I could see were faint shapes. Pumpkin shapes, house shapes, the shapes of tall, wide pine trees, and then the shape of something else. Something furry and wide. Something coming close, then closer. I closed my eyes tight and opened them again. I wiped my face with my sleeve and then wiped it all over again. The shape startled, then stilled. I was still too. I thought I might be dreaming.

Of course, I wasn't dreaming at all, but simply coming face-to-face with the Shetland pony from up the road. I'd seen him a few times before when he'd wander the outskirts of Miss Enid's farm and had made note of his peculiarly round shape.

The pony approached me slowly, closer and closer, until I could see the sopping bundle of gleaming whiskers on his long snout. He stared at me and I stared back.

His coat was long and shaggy, its soft growth coming in with the onset of fall. I knew that pony didn't have a name because old Miss Enid told me so. Miss Enid was the mean farmer lady who lived up the road from us and hissed at anyone who crossed her path. She told me that her pony beast had been given to her by a family that moved away. She told me that the beast ate everything in his line of sight, including her reading glasses, newspapers, and trash. Vegetables and flowers from her garden. A pitcher of iced tea left out on the front porch—part of the plastic pitcher included. Scotch tape. Wrapping paper. Cardboard boxes and the rims of rubber boots. A wooden sign advertising mums for sale. Mums too. She said the beast was evil and she had tried to sell him but to no avail. Apparently, no one was interested in buying an evil pony beast.

So there I was, drowning in the pouring rain, face-to-face with the beast himself. Eye to eye with a bushy monster, and when I say eye to eye, I mean eyes to eye. Even through the sheets of rain, I could see that the beast had only one eye. I had never noticed this before, since we had never been in such close contact. But it was abundantly clear: Old Miss Enid's pony beast had only a single eye, like the Cyclops from Crete. The massive creature stood before me, drenched, his mane soaking, one wide eye winking, the other gone.

Who knew if this monster bit or kicked or stampeded?

I shivered and leaned away.

The beast stepped forward, swung his dripping head,

then pounced on the pumpkin. Before I knew what was happening, his whole face disappeared into the soft orange skin. When it emerged, there was pulp dangling from the beast's long red pony whiskers.

I couldn't help but laugh.

But then I stopped. What was a girl to do? How would the beast find his way home, and how could I let cranky Miss Enid know that he was right there in my own front yard? As usual, my father was dead asleep in his bedroom and there was no one else around.

Pony beast, I whispered inside of my head, *go away. Go home.*

He didn't move, but nudged his big head closer to mine. I could see where the one eye might have once been, an eerily blank socket instead of a pupil and lid. The beast stank like nothing I had ever smelled before, and I sneezed.

I stood up, and the rain started to weaken like a giant faucet were slowly being turned off from above. Then the beast snorted and shook out his wet mane, spraying me with rainwater and pelts of pumpkin peel.

Gross.

Git, I thought, trying to stare him down. *Git.*

And what do you know? The beast looked right at me as if he understood. For a short moment, he nibbled at the nasty pumpkin remains with his lumpy lips and then turned his big self right around.

I watched as the pony trotted off, his long yellow tail

trailing behind like a flag of some kind. A pony flag representing the country of pony beasts. A world of pony beasts who ate pumpkin and had only one eye.

A stinky present graced my front walk as the beast traveled forward toward home, toward the pasture where Miss Enid didn't even know his name.

An hour later, he was back, and to my surprise he continued to visit me all through the day into evening, even after the pumpkin was gone and I kept shooing him away. In fact, I couldn't seem to get rid of this strange and stubborn creature. I'd spy his dense shape from far off, then the heavy sway of his head and body as he slowly trotted forward. His trot was slow, as if he found it difficult to move at all. And no wonder; this Shetland pony wasn't just plump—he was most definitely obese.

His coat was a reddish brown, his muzzle darker as if dipped in chocolate, and his mane and tail were light yellowy blond, close to white. He might have been a more attractive pony if his mane wasn't so matted and if he wasn't covered with mud and dust, dried grass and hay, remnants of tree branches and bits of bark. During one of his visits I found a long blue feather stuck to his rear and on the next a wad of bubble gum on his left hoof.

The pony was short, very short—probably no taller than four feet at the rump, excluding his huge head. I knew this because I could almost see over his ears, and according to the measuring stick I kept in kitchen broom closet, I was four feet, nine inches. Of course, it was sometime last year when I most recently measured myself, so there was no telling what my height really was.

I hadn't weighed myself for an even longer time, not since the school nurse completed my health chart in the third grade.

"Too thin," she muttered to herself when I stepped off the scale. "What have you been eating, anyway? Bread and water?"

Actually, I *had* been eating bread and water and was steamed that the nurse hit the nail on the head. My father brought home long packages of spongy white bread wrapped in cellophane printed with a red-and-blue-balloon pattern. The bread was so soft that I could mash it up into a kind of clay with bits of soft apple pulp and then roll it into small spongy balls. It tasted particularly good all scrunched up like this, and when eaten with a large glass or two of water, the bread balls filled up my belly so I wouldn't wake up hungry in the middle of the night.

The pony, however, had apparently eaten more than just bread. He was almost as round as he was tall, his enormous stomach sagging pitifully toward the ground.

"Shetland ponies have a tendency toward lameness from overeating," I remembered reading in a textbook last year during the stupid Know Your Animal Friends unit at school. "And it is essential that their weight be managed when not living in the wild. If not, they will quickly became dangerously overweight."

It became immediately clear that the textbook was correct. The Shetland that kept on appearing at my door didn't seem to care what he gobbled up, but would inhale everything in his path, including the sneaker that I'd left outside to dry after the rain and the stick of Juicy Fruit I'd been saving for later.

And so I could see from the get-go that Miss Enid was right about one thing: The pony beast was definitely devilish.

The Beast
Gets a Name

By Friday, the beast and I were becoming fast friends. I'd given up worrying about old Enid accusing me of horse thieving, since her pony kept returning to my house on his own, despite my attempts to shoo him home. I figured that in a court trial, should it come to that, I would most definitely be declared innocent.

A pony beast is not the typical companion for a mature eleven-year-old, and although I enjoyed his visits, I also had to overcome some of his shortcomings. First and foremost, he was the filthiest animal I had seen in my entire life. His coat was always caked with mud, as if he'd bathed in it on purpose, something I soon found out to be close to the actual truth.

This pony adored dirt. He rolled in it, ate it, spewed it in dusty billows, pawed it, licked it, became it. Dirt was a perfect name for him, and it wasn't long before he learned to respond when I called him from way inside my head.

Impossible? I thought so too.

At first I could hardly believe it, that this misshapen critter could actually understand my thoughts, without my speaking them aloud. After all, I was a pretty logical girl with my feet planted firmly on the ground. I didn't believe in magic, in the supernatural, or in the dumb horoscopes that all the girls at Robert Frost loved to giggle over. They would bunch up together around one person, usually that simpering Lavinia T. Stout, and listen to her read about how she would soon become famous and find the love of her life, all according to her stupid birth sign and the stars and planets.

Dumb and dumber.

So believing that a one-eyed, filthy pony could read my mind was quite a stretch for me, and it took a few days until I really came to terms with the idea at all. I most certainly wasn't an idiot, and knew that Dirt couldn't really know what I was thinking because of some stupid hocus-pocus, but because he grew to know me. He stared at me with his one eye, sniffed me up and down, listened for every breath. If I inhaled sharply, he stopped in his tracks. If I bowed my head, he bowed his too, or pressed against me with a warm flank. If I was worried and chewed my nails nervously, his ears shot upright.

If I thought about my mother and sighed, he gently nibbled my neck and then made me laugh by tickling my palm with his bouquet of whiskers, prickly but delicate as dandelion stems.

Sometimes logic doesn't make sense, although I know that's a contradiction in terms. And by the Sunday after my suspension, there was little doubt. Dirt could hear me, although I didn't speak.

Example one:

On Saturday morning, I tripped on the front stairs to my own house and skinned my left knee all the way through my pants. Of course I didn't cry—I'm simply not the sniveling type—but blood seemed to be oozing everywhere, and for a minute I thought I might pass out. While I'm pretty tough when it comes to most things, the sight of blood does make me feel a touch woozy, so I sat myself right down on the steps, lowering my head between my knees. The scrape stung like crazy and I tried to remember if we had any Band-Aids in the house. Probably not.

I couldn't help but think of my mother then, of how she might have patched me up with a bit of ointment and a clean white bandage, gently brushing the hair out of my eyes and curving her arm around my shoulders. She might have kissed me on the top of my head and told me how much she loved me. She would have cared that I hurt myself, no matter how small the wound.

And so I wished for my mother to be there then, something I tried to never do. I tried not to let myself ever wish for her or remember how it felt to have her by my side when I was hurting or how it felt for her fingers to brush my cheek in tiny strokes. She always said that those were butterfly kisses of the fingertips.

Then it happened. Something warm and damp actually did brush the top of my forehead. I looked up quickly. But instead of smelling my mother's burnt-sugar-and-maple-syrup scent, I inhaled that of wood chips and mulch.

Dirt had mysteriously appeared from who knows where without a sound, and was dropping his mangy head down to mine. Of course, it might have just been a coincidence, but it seemed as though this ridiculous figure of a pony was actually trying to comfort me, as though he knew that I was hurting and that I was missing my mother.

I raised one hand to pat his slobbery snout, my head still lowered, and then he responded in kind, rubbing his whole muzzle over one of my cheeks and then the other.

If anything was to make me teary, it would have been this: an animal's soft, soggy touch against my cold skin.

Example two:

The very next day, Sunday, I was climbing a rotten apple tree behind the little crooked house, something I knew was a bad idea from the start. While apple trees aren't very tall and don't present a danger of falling extremely far, this one was unusually big and hadn't sprouted anything that looked like an apple or a leaf for over a year or so. So I knew there was a possibility that the branches were dead and wouldn't hold me, and yet I couldn't resist shimmying up the short trunk and then stepping gingerly all the way to the top, where I'd spied a small bird's nest. It's not a good idea for nests to be so exposed to the elements, and the babies could be scooped up by birds of prey when not under cover. And there wasn't a speck of cover on that apple tree; not a sprout, not a single dot of green.

My father taught me to climb trees a long time ago. He'd told me not to tell my mother about our climbing adventures since she probably wouldn't have approved. So we'd sneak out to the backyard and run toward the very same apple tree that I was climbing now, except that it was healthy back then, its branches firm and its trunk solid. My father and I would swing our legs up over the low-lying branches and together reach up above. But I was just a little kid then, and couldn't make it very far. So my father would swoop me into his arms and slide me over his broad back. And up the tree we'd go, me hanging on piggyback style, and my father's strong arms pulling us higher and higher.

But that was when my mother was still alive.

When I reached the top of the apple tree and stretched out my hand to bring the nest to safety, I quickly realized that my own well-being was at risk. Crack, crack; I heard one branch snap under me, and then another.

I was stranded up top, hanging on to a swiftly weakening, fragile piece of bark. To call it a branch would be an overstatement. And then, just as I was preparing myself for an uncomfortable fall to the hard ground, I spied the yellow mane of my pony tangled in the lower branches below.

He neighed unhappily, as if to complain, then carefully raised his craggy head to stare up at me with one glaring eye. Was it possible that Dirt was displeased with me for my foolish decision to climb so weak a tree? Certainly not. A pony couldn't, wouldn't think that way. Was it possible that he knew I was in distress and came to rescue me? Possibly. I knew it was crazy, but possibly.

He braced his thick haunches and neighed again, then shook his head wildly. Luckily for me, more branches snapped off around him, just as they had fallen under my weight a few minutes before, clearing an escape path. I tried to reach down but slipped.

Ouch.

Sliding down a rough tree trunk is never a good idea,

and I felt it scratch every inch of skin under my T-shirt until I pressed my knees against the bark as tightly as possible. Steadying myself, I held on to my one poor excuse for a branch with my right hand and stretched all the way below with the other to grasp Dirt's thick forelock. Quickly releasing the branch, I next encircled his neck with both arms and dropped all the way down. Whoosh. For a moment, I was sitting on Dirt the way a rider might mount a horse, except I was backward, facing his rump instead of his head. He didn't move; he didn't even twitch. It wasn't until I was back on the ground again that he shook out his whole burly body, just like he'd been swimming in the Shelter pond, and then his sweet head. Was he reprimanding me for my mistake?

I guess I was going crazy after all. But if crazy was becoming friends with a pony who understood me, I was okay with it.

My Delinquency Is Discovered

Social workers are different from police officers. They aren't allowed to carry guns.

Good thing.

Ms. Trudy Trumpet, a social worker from the Shelter Department of Child and Family Services, first came to my house on Monday at about ten a.m., almost a full week after Principal Flint's suspension. I had been enjoying my extended suspension so much, I thought I might just stretch it into the following week, and certainly didn't expect a visitor.

It didn't take me too long to learn that Trudy didn't care about what I expected.

She stood outside my front door, chewing gum and looking down apprehensively at her own right foot.

"Hello, Yonder," she said, without hardly looking up.

"My name is Trudy Trumpet and I'm from social services. We're concerned about your missing school."

Her frizzy black hair was twisted into two short braids that stood out on either side of her head, pointing in opposite directions. A sequined cap topped curly bangs in a crown, its visor turned to one side. She stood there for a few minutes, then quickly jerked up her foot in a clumsy effort to see the bottom of her shoe. Ms. Trudy Trumpet's foot was tiny and seemed delicate held up to her considerable chest. She was wearing black leather sneakers with hot-pink shoelaces. I wondered if those laces were regulation.

I shrugged coolly, and she shrugged back.

I sighed and then she sighed.

Then she pointed to her one shoe, lifted it so that I could see the sole covered in pony poop, and pretended to gag.

I couldn't help but snicker.

She snickered too.

That first time, Trudy didn't come all the way into the house. Instead she just stuck her head inside and asked me if I was okay.

"I'm Trudy Trumpet," she said all over again, "and have been assigned your case. Hear you're not going to school these days. You all right?"

I nodded. I thought Trudy looked strange, but not exactly weirdo strange, just short and plump as a gnome. She smiled, and her grin glistened. Her skin was the color of apple cider, and her face a perfect circle.

"No trouble with your father or anything else? I hear that you're an A student with a history of pretty good attendance. Anything I can help you with?"

I shook my head and put a hand to my head, indicating fever.

"Sick?"

I nodded.

"Okay, then." She took a deep breath, clearly relieved, and then I noticed her green, green eyes. "There's a nasty flu going round, so you take care of yourself, but I really don't know why those folks in admin insisted I come all the way out here when you're just missing school from illness. Can't help it if you're sick."

I raised my eyebrows just a bit.

"Your teachers will be expecting you, Yonder," Trudy continued, drawing back her shoulders and shaking her head. "Make sure that they aren't disappointed and that there aren't any more absences once you're feeling better. Not a single one, okay? And it looks to me as though you're recovering pretty well."

I didn't nod then, but shook Trudy's plump, warm hand as she reached out to me that very first visit.

It was the very next day when Trudy reappeared.

"Gotta horse stowed away somewhere?" she asked

before I had a chance to look up from relaxing on my front steps. "My gram used to have an old mare when I was raised up."

Horse? How in heaven's name did Trudy know I'd been hanging out with a pony? Then I remembered her stepping in Dirt dung.

She was wearing a baby-blue knit beret this time, despite the early September warmth. Her braids fanned out in front of her ears, creating the illusion of sideburns.

Dirt was indulging in his morning siesta out back, and I had been taking a break from pony patrol to scratch the seven mosquito bites that lined both of my ankles with a stick. They itched like crazy.

Trudy sat down beside me, and her bubble-gum scent swished over me. I felt a bit nauseated.

"Hey, Yonder," she said softly, almost as if talking to herself. "You doing okay?"

What business was it of hers?

Trudy didn't say anything just then, but slowly pried the mosquito stick from my hands and bent over, writing something in the dried dirt. One of her stiff braids brushed my right cheek, startling me so that I gulped and then coughed. Trudy's eyes were slits as she examined my suspicious face solemnly.

"You really sick again today?" she asked. "The school thinks that you're faking it. No phone call from you father."

I stopped coughing. I wished that the woman would

29

pack up her baby-blue beret and pink shoelaces and hit the streets.

MY NAME IS TRUDY, she wrote in the ground in front of us with my very own stick. I'M HERE TO HELP.

It wasn't as if I were deaf, for goodness' sake. It wasn't necessary to write letters in the ground. I had two ears.

Trudy scratched in the sandy soil again. HOW CAN I HELP?

I shrugged and looked down. I may have rolled my eyes.

Trudy prodded my knee with the stick and then handed it to me as if I'd asked. I noticed that her fingernails were long and shiny, their tips filed into squares and painted bright white. I thought they looked dumb.

"You're sure you're okay?"

I nodded.

"Still feeling sick? Nothing you want to talk about? You know, I'm here to help."

I shrugged again.

"Well, then. Well." She stood up slowly, brushing off the dust on her knees and wiping away all traces of the message she had left in the dirt. "If you're absolutely sure. It's time for my lunch, anyway, and there's no use sitting around whiling away the entire day when there are other children to see and triple-decker hamburgers to eat. Now, get your stuff together and be sure you head out to school first thing in the morning or I'm going to have to visit your father at his place of work and send in an official report."

The idea of lunch distracted me for a moment. It couldn't have been later than ten o'clock, and I didn't know any actual adult who ate lunch before noon.

"Want to join me for something to eat?" Trudy asked, lightly laying her palm on my shoulder. I shivered.

"Yonder? Did you hear my question? It's not just anyone I invite to join me for a chow-down. Want to keep me company down at the Mutter Street Grill and do some damage on a burger and fries? You look like you could use a good meal to put some meat on your bones." Trudy looked into my face, but I was almost scared of what she might see, what she might find out. That I hadn't eaten anything at all the whole day. That the day before all I had was four balls of bread and three apples. That the idea of a meal made me insane with yearning. That the words *burger and fries* were the most tempting words I had ever heard in my whole entire life. That no one in my recent memory had ever invited me to lunch, or any meal for that matter. But of course, I didn't respond.

I looked away back toward the house.

I didn't need charity and I sure didn't need Trudy.

But Trudy clearly wasn't concentrating on me or my house. She just grunted, and hitched up her pants like an old man. She shot me a solemn sideways glance.

"Well, okay," she said. "Up to you, I suppose. Guess I'll be eating alone. You sure?"

I nodded.

"You gonna get going to school tomorrow?"

I nodded again.

"Promise?"

I nodded for the third time, knowing that each nod was an enormous lie, a lie that would probably catch up to me before I had a chance to make it the truth.

"Okay, then. I'm counting on you, girl," she said, and then looked away.

And before I knew what was what and before I could think anymore, Trudy had left my side. I watched as she shuffled back down the little path from my door all the way into the mess of tall pine trees that guarded us from the road.

I stood up and watched until Trudy disappeared—a dim shape drifting downhill.

Trudy the Terrible

Wednesday morning, the third time Trudy Trumpet came to my house, she was not happy. She was not smiling or the least friendly; she wasn't teasing me about Dirt dung or writing me nice notes in the ground. In fact, she looked pretty annoyed.

"Yonder," Trudy said, as soon as I answered the door despite myself, "enough is enough. It's time to go to school and there's no two ways about it. I told you that you had one more chance before I took things into my own hands and reported to my supervisor, and if that happens, I don't know what. You surely don't want that kind of trouble. I thought you and I had an understanding. Now, please get your things together and let's go. My supervisor will be miffed, and I'm losing patience with your insubordination."

I didn't like the sound of the word *miffed*. There aren't

very many words that I don't like, but *miffed* is most definitely one of them.

Trudy had chosen a red pillbox hat to wear that morning; it was embossed with black felt design. I thought it was kind of fetching

She tapped her pink-shoelaced foot impatiently, munching on what looked like strawberry chewing gum. I could spy a sliver of color in her mouth. I wondered about that gum. I wondered if she had any more and if I might nab a piece. My stomach gurgled.

"Yonder?"

I stood there for a moment, trying not to panic but carefully weighing my options. On the one hand, I could most certainly outrun Trudy; on the other hand, she could always call for backup if I tried to leave the scene.

But going back to Robert Frost Middle School wasn't a good option either. I'd already decided that.

So I ended up doing what I did best: pretending not to understand. Tricking Trudy by making her think that my brain was muddled. In other words, I played dumb.

"Yonder!" Trudy said again, this time clearly agitated. "Let's go. Get your stuff together and I'll walk you there myself. Tried to find your father up at the orchard earlier this morning, drove all the way to Holler Hollow, but he must have been out in the fields somewhere."

What Trudy didn't know was that my father was passed out in his own room. I couldn't let her find him. Social services might be picky about his sleeping throughout the day and take me away from my own home. I had read enough stories about this. I knew the score.

Was it my imagination or did Trudy's braids begin to curl upward as she became more and more aggravated?

"Yonder, did you hear me? It's time for school. Right now. You know, you can't keep on living on your own island in this little house. The rest of the world is out there just waiting for you, so get off your bottom and make it quick." Then she continued by muttering to herself: "You'd think by now . . ." And "I don't understand these children . . ." And "I'm getting too old for this nonsense."

I was getting more and more aggravated myself. My options were seriously limited, and I wasn't one to do well with limitations. Trudy was making a fuss right in front of me, but the idea of going back to school where I was teased by stupid kids and ignored by dumb teachers didn't thrill me. On the other hand, simply ignoring Trudy Trumpet wasn't possible.

Trudy was tapping her foot at the door all over again. Beads of sweat glistened on her cheeks. I wondered why social services hadn't given her better training—it was clear she hadn't been adequately prepared to work with challenging situations or with children as determined as me. But reaching for my mother's old khaki jacket and rubbing my eyes with my fists in a gesture of fatigue, I closed the front door behind me and followed Trudy to the road.

Luckily for me, Robert Frost Middle School was only a few blocks from my house, so I didn't have to listen to Trudy's lecturing for too long as we walked down Mutter Street, then Clucker, then Yelle. Actually, Trudy walked and I shuffled, dragging one foot behind the other.

"Put a hitch in your giddyup, girl!" she'd say every few steps. "You're already late. Come on, Yonder, you can move faster than that."

The later the better, I thought. Fortunately, it was Wednesday and school let out early for teacher meetings, so I wouldn't have to endure too many hours of torture. And the fact that Dirt wouldn't get his lunchtime constitutional, something I had just started, wasn't too much of a problem since I'd be back in a few hours. I'd recently begun Dirt on an exercise schedule that included a few trots around the house. Sometimes, he seemed to appreciate my efforts to trim down his physique, but sometimes, he refused to move. He was definitely a stubborn pony.

When we arrived at the school's entryway, I briefly thought about bolting but reconsidered when I scanned the horizon for a way out. I knew that Trudy wasn't the type to give up easily; even if I was able to slip away, she'd most likely appear at my doorstep the minute I got home. And so, like an escapee returning to prison, I finally skulked regretfully through Robert Frost's front door.

Mr. Rosen in the office gave me a late slip to bring to class, glaring over his thick tortoiseshell-framed glasses, but to my surprise and delight my class was taking a test on Greek gods, something I could ace without even trying. Ms. Wang passed a test paper to my desk and smiled.

"Glad you're feeling better, Yonder," she said, patting my arm. Ms. Wang was usually soft-spoken and pretty nice, not the typical Robert Frost teacher. She told us that she was born in Beijing, China, which I found interesting, and I admired her gleaming black hair worn bobbed at the shoulder. I would have given anything to have hair like Ms. Wang's instead of my wild red curls. When Ms. Wang turned her head, her hair swung and then fell right back into place perfectly. Whenever I even shifted position, my hair seemed to sprout new cowlicks, making me look like a poodle with static electricity. Not that I really cared much about my appearance, but cowlicks are straight-up embarrassing.

Poor Ms. Wang sure didn't know how to control a class of fifth-grade savages and never seemed to see how I was tortured from morning to afternoon. But I knew that she was probably thrilled to have me back since I was one of her most well-behaved students and many of the other kids didn't even bother to listen in class.

As soon as the test was over, things returned to normal. Heywood Prune, gloating at me from across the room, offered to collect the papers and return them to Ms. Wang's desk. When she was busy writing on the blackboard with her favorite yellow chalk, ole Prune started up with me all over again.

I smelled the odor of corn chips, noticed a single pistachio nut slowly rolling across the floor, and felt my stomach tighten.

Of course, I was minding my very own business, sitting at my own stupid desk, drawing on my arm with a red Magic Marker, when wham, old Prune suddenly walked by and whacked me on the head with a book. Then, before I knew what was what, he pulled open the back of my collar and dropped something down my shirt. I bolted upright, shaking my shirt until a squashed stinkbug dropped out. The entire class laughed. When Ms. Wang looked up, Prune flashed a bright smile and bent over with a flourish and uneven bow.

The rest of the day went pretty okay. Prune and his friends were pathetic dancers so I felt good in performing arts as I breezed through the Virginia reel without a stumble. And when Prune tried to trip me during "Spin your partner round and round," Mr. Tisdale made him sit in the corner for a time-out. Now it was my turn to smirk. Math and science also weren't too bad either since Prune and his best friend, Ethan Diggs, hadn't done their homework and were sent to study hall.

Then, to my surprise, Principal Flint asked me to stay after school later than usual, to help plan for the book fair, which was coming at the end of the month. I looked forward to the book fair every year, and Principal Flint sometimes asked me to help her pick out books to order. She knew I loved to read and thought I'd make good choices.

All in all, I figured I got off pretty easy this first day back at school. Not too much stress or drama. I raced home as quickly as possible, finding the front door all the way open and a bit off-kilter.

Something wasn't right, and I immediately smelled trouble.

While my father and I never locked the front door, we always pulled it tightly shut so Walt Whitman, the town stray dog, wouldn't weasel his way in and eat the vinyl right off our kitchen floor. Walt Whitman was extremely fond of vinyl.

I threw my knapsack across the living room, then skidded to a sudden stop. The living room couch and chair were overturned and my collection of library books was strewn across the floor.

Clear signs of a struggle. Evidence of a brawl.

My heart stopped.

Had we been robbed? Not that there was anything of value in the little crooked house. Had my father been kidnapped or picked up by the police for driving while drinking? It wouldn't be the first time.

But then I heard a familiar sputter coming from the kitchen and smelled a familiar scent. A trail of hay led from the living room to the kitchen. And a trail of poop as well, perhaps left to show me the way.

Dirt looked proud of himself when I found him drinking from my father's special cider pan, left in the kitchen sink. His ears were flopped back, a sign of supreme pony relaxation; he bobbed his head, rubbed his cheek against the kitchen counter, and then raised his tail in pure pony scorn. Then, right in front of my eyes, Dirt had the nerve to drop three big ones directly onto the kitchen floor.

I couldn't believe it. First, my pony rudely let himself into the house without an invitation, and next, he left behind smelly evidence of his visit. He knew better. I was irritated, to say the least.

Dirt and I stared at each other in mutual contempt: he for my coming home late from school, and me for his breaking into the house uninvited. I knew that Enid tied my pony up outside at night and that he'd probably never had a stable or real home. But pushing his way into my house seemed disrespectful.

Dirt, I told him, *I think it's time for us to make a pact. Your life's been hard, but now we have each other, so let's both try our best. I promise to take good care of you, but you've got to pay attention and behave. That's what a pact is, a promise to each other.*

He stomped one hoof and then another, letting out a blustery sigh. I could see by the forward position of his ears that he was still holding a grudge.

Come here. Here, Dirt.

He wriggled slowly toward me, head downward, as if

unsure whether to come forward or bolt away, but when I stretched out my hand, he nipped it gently. It was a gentle, friendly nip, so I knew that he understood.

Dirt, I told him, *I'm sorry that I was late today, but I'm doing the best that I can. It's going to be lonely for you when I'm at school, but hang in there. I'll try to make it home to keep you company a bit earlier in the future. And maybe we can build you a lean-to one day soon, somewhere warm and dry to call your own.*

But Dirt's intake of special cider had made him a bit tipsy, and by the time I raised my head to look him in his one eye, my pony was dead asleep, still standing upright on all four legs.

Dirt's Secret Is Revealed

The days and weeks at Robert Frost passed slowly, but I still saw Dirt every afternoon. I would race home after PE, and there he'd be, waiting for me, lazily sunning himself in the September sunshine or napping contentedly, spread out on the dead grass in front of the little crooked house. The first time I saw him lying there, I was alarmed, not realizing that horses and ponies sometimes slept prone instead of standing upright. The sight of Dirt snoring away on the ground was frightening.

But he was fine, as always, peering up to grin at me with those thick dark-pink lips and exposing those enormous yellow teeth. His goofy grins always made me laugh.

And every day, I became more and more convinced that

what I had imagined about Dirt understanding me was actually real.

He listened to my voice without hearing any words.

Voice is different than speech, although most people think it's the same. It's what you feel and mean instead of what you say. Your voice is who you really are, not who you pretend to be.

But it's easy to be overlooked when you don't speak aloud. Folks think you're stupid or don't know your own mind. And yet Dirt seemed to hear me clearly despite it all.

Dirt, come! I would wish, and he would head my way.

Dirt, stop! I sometimes shouted silently, and he'd usually stop, raising his head wearily as if to tell me he was extremely bored and only cooperating out of obligation. But eventually, he would comply, even if it took a minute or two.

Amazingly, astonishingly.

Wanna treat? I'd wonder, hoping for silky pony whiskers to tickle my palm. Dirt's whiskers, his soft purplish-pink lips, felt good against my skin, and I often found myself yearning for his touch.

I began to think about Dirt each night as I was trying to fall asleep during those long September evenings. The last summer fireflies would still be out, bumping the glass, silently asking to be let inside, but the promise of winter—I could never wait for the first snow—slid crisp breezes through my drafty window. Instead of staying awake and fretting about my father's special cider, Heywood Prune, and Robert Frost Middle School, I would fret about my pony. I started to wonder where he slept, what he ate for dinner, if he found his way back home after an afternoon visit with me, and if irritable Enid knew how to care for him the way he deserved to be cared for.

Why did I grow to like Dirt so much and so quickly? Hard to say. It wasn't as though he was cuddly or sweet. He wasn't a pretty animal, if horses are ever pretty, and he sure wasn't pleasant. His one good eye often glared at me, as if I were responsible for all of his problems. And his size made it difficult for him to trot or even walk gracefully.

Dirt liked to stand still a lot, sniffing for things to shove in his mouth, sometimes sticking his nose under my jacket. He liked to nip and loved to trick me by slowly rolling in a puddle and splashing until every inch of my pants and shirt was wet. If I tried to run away, he would follow, shaking off water every step of the way and finally laying his sopping-wet pony head on my shoulder.

Sometimes Dirt smelled like straw, like wet grass, like meadow. But more often he smelled like other things, not particularly pleasant. His yellow mane was rough to the touch, but his coat was slick and soft that early fall, soon to thicken, long and downy as pussy willow. A ridge of dark-amber-and-white-speckled fringe grew up from hooves to haunch and then again down from his chin to his throat and all the way across his broad chest. He was solid and not at all spongy underneath, despite his girth—when you leaned against his rump and rubbed his bulging belly, he didn't feel soft like I'd imagined. Dirt was dense as rock.

He never looked away when I leaned against him in moments of unspoken friendship. He didn't ply me with endless questions or make judgments about how I looked, my name, that I didn't speak, the fact that my father drank and drank and drank and didn't really know how to be a regular father at all. Dirt didn't care about my not going to school or the four-room crooked frame house where my father was sleeping his life away. Dirt didn't care that I locked my father's bedroom door each and every evening at seven p.m. so he wouldn't forget where he was, who he was, that he even had a daughter at all. So he wouldn't forget all of it and stumble away. Out of his room, out of the kitchen, out the door and down the front steps. So I wouldn't lose him the way I lost my mother.

Dirt didn't care. Dirt didn't care about any of it.

And I came to see that Dirt was a brave pony, for the most part. When a truck blared loudly from down Mutter Street or Bellow Avenue, I was surprised that he didn't rear up the way a regular horse might. He didn't seem scared of me when I tried to shoo him home; he wasn't skittish about mosquitoes, flies, bumblebees, neighborhood dogs barking, or anything that you might expect a pony to fear.

I worried about every last thing for Dirt, but came to

discover that there was one thing and one thing alone that terrified him.

One warm late September afternoon when Dirt was visiting, I found out his secret by accident. I was filling an old plastic flower planter with water from the garden hose so my pony could have a cool drink. Dirt had spent the last hour nibbling on front-yard weeds and I thought he might be thirsty. But when I reached for the hose, he let out a high-pitched sound, not quite a neigh and not quite a scream. I dropped it immediately, and he settled. I reached for the hose again and Dirt's one eye rolled back in his head. He skirted backward.

All I had to do was just touch the hose and that nervous Nellie would immediately swing up his old head and start his silly backward dance. I quickly kicked the hose under a deep pile of leaves.

It's okay, Dirt. See? The hose is gone. It's all okay now.

He approached me slowly, one step at a time. I could see that his neck was damp and he was panting.

All gone. No need to be scared. Here, Dirt, come here.

I held up both hands to show that they were empty. Knowing that I'd frightened him somehow frightened me. What if I'd lost his trust? My eyes filled up and my throat closed at the thought.

Then, I swear and cross my heart, Dirt trotted forward and laid his giant, matted head on my shoulder and nuzzled my ear. When I turned to pat him, our lips brushed in a surprising, messy pony kiss. Maybe some folks would think this disgusting, and even I might consider kissing a pony on the mouth kind of gross. But it isn't often that an animal tries to thank you for saving him, so gross or not, I waited until Dirt turned his head away again before wiping my mouth with the back of my hand.

After all, even a pony can have his feelings hurt.

Delivering Dirt
from Danger

I had never planned for Dirt to move in with me. It wasn't as if I wanted to give up my small bedroom to his big butt. And there sure wasn't any extra space in my little crooked house.

But when I saw the wooden sign planted at the end of Enid's driveway during my evening walk in search of old pumpkins, I thought I might just pass out cold then and there on the side of the road.

My stomach churned at the sight of the slanted slab of wood, a sign sloppily painted with six red words. For a minute, I thought I was having a nightmare and pinched my arm just to be sure.

It couldn't be.

PONY FOR SALE.
GOOD-QUALITY HORSEMEAT.

Horsemeat and *pony* should never appear in the same sentence.

My blood ran cold at the thought. I knew that horsemeat was often sold somewhere on the outskirts of town; Heywood Prune told me this last year during Know Your Animal Friends Week. While Prune may have just been trying to tease me, I couldn't get the terrible image of a horsemeat-sausage factory out of my head. Horrifying.

Old Enid was mean, but she couldn't be cruel enough to do the unthinkable, could she? I read the red painted words all over again. There was no doubt.

Dirt had become a pony with a bounty on his head.

I sped over to evil Enid's warped wooden sign and pulled it out of the ground. Then I scrambled all the way home, scanning the horizon for any sign of Dirt. What if he'd already been caught and sent to the you-know-where?

What if I never got to see him again?

I ran without passing a single person, the wooden sign leaving splinters in my hands. If Enid or anyone else saw me dashing down the road with a horsemeat sign clutched in my arms, I'd be in hot water. And hot water was exactly what I needed to avoid if I was to protect my pony from harm.

I was Dirt's one and only friend, and he was mine.

When I finally made it home, Dirt was there, rudely

rooting around the new pumpkin on my front steps, just as though he'd received a personal invitation. He looked up at my arrival. A narrow piece of white plastic, perhaps gnawed from a corner of Enid's lemonade pitcher, hung from his mouth like a giant cigarette. His one eye glistened, and he bobbed his enormous head up and down in a proud pony greeting. To my surprise and amusement, half of his heft was actually hidden backward, all the way inside my little crooked house, while his front half proudly revealed itself in the afternoon sun. It was evident that this rude pony had backed himself through my front doorway to have better access to his pumpkin snack.

Darn it, Dirt, I thought, so relieved that I was angry. *Darn it—don't you have any manners? Don't you know it's not polite for a pony to wedge his rear into someone's home?*

And the idea came to me just like that.

Brilliant!

I'd rescue Dirt from danger. I'd make sure that he was never scooped up by any horsemeat factory and would never have to return to Enid's grasp. I'd hide and protect him.

I'd move Dirt into my house.

All of a sudden, I realized that it was late in the day and my father might be awake. What if he noticed that a three-hundred-pound pony had parked himself halfway into our house? I wasn't sure that he'd be pleased.

I shot ahead and started inside, gently smacking Dirt's muzzle so he'd let me through.

Polite as a pony can be, he pirouetted backward and I nudged myself in the door.

Out, I instructed him. *Out the door now!*

Just as I'd thought, my father was wide awake, sitting at the kitchen table with a big mug of his special cider. He nodded at me and grinned.

I grinned back, dropping the horsemeat sign on the floor. While I wasn't used to my father sitting at the table the way other fathers might wait for their dinners, I was happy to see him upright.

"Well." My father raised his eyebrows and took a long sip from his cup. Then he winked.

I tried to wink back but my eyelid got stuck midway.

"I see you have a new friend, darlin'."

I shrugged. Had my father noticed that Dirt's enormous backside had been crammed into our house just a few moments earlier?

Then my father laughed and pointed.

Apparently, Dirt had chosen to ignore my instructions and follow me all the way into the house without my knowing. Now wasn't the proper time to remind him of his manners, but I was definitely annoyed and turned myself around to give him my most critical look.

Dirt smacked his lips.

"Who's your buddy?" My father stood up from the table, swaying from side to side, then sat down again. "Nice lookin' animal, but what's it doing in the house?"

I ignored the question and slid my arm around Dirt's neck, resting my cheek on his nape. My father would have to understand the urgency, the danger Dirt was in.

"The both of you look like two peas in a pod." My father smiled.

I nodded. Dirt may have nodded too, but I felt like crying.

"You okay, darlin'?" My father looked alarmed.

I shrugged, looking down so he wouldn't see my face. I wanted my father to understand the importance of saving Dirt, but I didn't want him to see me cry.

"Hey, wait a minute. Hey, wait a sec." My father stood up again, this time straight and steady. "This isn't the pony old Enid's trying to sell, is it? Why, the boys at the orchard were talking about it, that she's selling her pony for horsemeat."

I may have sniffled. I looked at my father imploringly.

He walked over to where I was standing and rubbed Dirt's muzzle as if he had been rubbing pony muzzles for his whole life. Dirt's entire body quivered with delight.

"Well, we won't have it, will we, Yonder girl? We can't allow this fine figure of a horse to be sent upriver. I wish I had the money to pay for him."

I knew we were short on cash. But we were always short on cash, and this time, I just didn't care. I didn't care about anything but saving Dirt.

"Maybe we could keep him out back for a time?" My father combed his long salt-and-pepper hair with his fingers. "I could tie him to that old apple tree until I save enough from the orchard to pay Enid."

I shook my head vehemently. No pony of mine was going to be kept outside tied to a rotten apple tree, particularly with winter coming. And anyway, anybody could spy him behind our house out there in the wide open. That would be serious trouble for us and even worse trouble for Dirt.

Dirt started nibbling at my father's belt. I felt my father's huge hand stroke my head slowly.

"Can't bear to see my girl unhappy," he said softly. "You've had enough of that to last a lifetime. If this here pony can make my Yonder girl smile, well, then we'll do what needs to be done. Any ideas, darlin'?"

I nodded quickly and pointed to my bedroom. *He can live there*, I thought, looking at my father plaintively.

His eyes widened. Dirt rubbed his nose against my father's hand.

"In the house?" my father asked incredulously.

I nodded again.

"Well," he drawled slow as molasses, a technique my father used when not wanting to give me an answer, "well, I never heard of such a thing."

My heart dropped. There were many things unheard of in my life. Why was this the time to draw the line? It was unheard of that I was teased unmercifully at school and unheard of that my father spent half of his life now with a glass of cider in his hand. It was unheard of that my mother wasn't there to understand.

I took both of my father's hands in my own and squeezed. I pressed my face into his chest.

"Yonder," he said, hugging me. "You know I'd do anything for my girl, but . . ."

I dropped his hands and threw myself onto a kitchen chair, burying my head in my arms. I may have been a tad overly dramatic. But this was a matter of life or death. If you're going to be overly dramatic, life or death seemed like good reasons.

Dirt snuffled.

My father cleared his throat. "Well," he drawled again, "well, now, I surely don't like to see you all upset, Yonder, but I just really don't know. It's not that I don't like animals, but moving a horse inside is a bit much—kinda crazy, don't you think?"

I shook my head.

"Come on, darlin', let's be sensible."

I shook my head again. *Sensible* wasn't in my vocabulary when it came to Dirt.

My father sighed.

I could tell that I was wearing him down. He never had much endurance.

"Craziest thing I've ever heard, but I suppose it's okay if you figure out how to take care of him and clean up after him. Not work for the fainthearted, darlin'. Just for a short while, now, Yonder. Just for a day or so. Thinking about it some, I remember that I had a pet turtle myself once. But that was long ago. A long, long time ago." My father staggered in place for a minute, and I saw his eyes glaze over the way they did when he needed to rest. "Hey, darlin', would you mind helping your old dad back to bed? And bring me a cold one from the refrigerator if it's not too much trouble. Gotta get some rest if I'm going to make it over to the orchard in the morning."

It was still late afternoon. The sun hadn't even started to set.

And yet, my father had agreed to the unagreeable. I felt my entire face beam. My pony and I were going to live together under the same roof.

How to Care for a Horse in the House

Imagine sneaking over three hundred pounds of hide and hair into your house.

Imagine that this hunk of heaven is a pony from the Shetland Islands.

Welcome to my world.

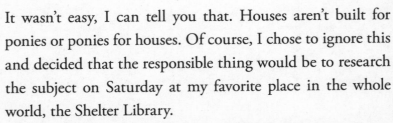

It wasn't easy, I can tell you that. Houses aren't built for ponies or ponies for houses. Of course, I chose to ignore this and decided that the responsible thing would be to research the subject on Saturday at my favorite place in the whole world, the Shelter Library.

The Shelter Library is small, studded with gleaming stone

on the outside and lined with worn cherrywood inside. Maybe it's all that wood that makes me dizzy, but every time I step through the door and inhale that familiar fragrance, my head starts to spin and my heart beats just a little bit faster. No kidding. There's a whoosh of dust mixed with orange oil and book perfume. What's book perfume? I'm not sure, but I do know that there's nothing else like it: yellowing paper, crumbling bindings, the scent of adventure and mystery.

And then there's the quiet. The library is the perfect place for someone who doesn't speak. The library's silence stuns me each and every time; not a word is spoken except for whispering now and then, but the shelves and shelves of books quake with questions and answers. Sentences shudder. Whole paragraphs pant.

I love the Shelter Library and that Ms. Alcott, the librarian, is never surprised to see me, but nods with a smidgen of a smile when I come in. Ms. Alcott is pretty old, probably around forty, with a mound of impressive orange dreadlocks that swing and clatter each time she moves. It must be the little purple beads sewn at the end that make that clattering sound—kind of nice. She usually wears purple sweaters and purple tights too. When Ms. Alcott stands up from behind her desk, all kinds of papers and files flutter to the floor. She seems flustered then, but never annoyed, stretching out her long arms to recover what has fallen without looking down. Ms. Alcott understands that I'm not one to make a sound, and that must be a relief since she's always telling folks to quiet down.

The town library has one computer, but I thought I should begin my studies the old-fashioned way, with an actual book. There's nothing like holding library books in your hands, especially the old ones with leather bindings and crisp tissue in between the illustrations. Each page feels like you're opening a present.

While the library had a number of books on horse care, there were only two specific to Shetlands. The first, a paperback with a dumb drawing of a horse wearing a flowered hat, didn't appeal to me, but the other fit the bill to perfection.

It was a large book, not leather bound, yet with a heavy canvas cover that felt substantial as I pulled it from the shelf. You always want to make sure that you have substantial books when doing important research. The volume, titled *Taking Care of Your Shetland* by Helen Muet, was published in 1980, so was unfortunately not in the category of books containing tissue-covered illustrations.

Still, Ms. Muet seemed to know her business, and I was able to gather quite a bit of useful information.

This is what I learned from studying *Taking Care of Your Shetland* by Helen Muet:

1. The Shetland Islands are part of the United Kingdom of Great Britain and Northern Ireland.

2. Shetland ponies need space to graze outside, but they shouldn't eat too much grass, otherwise they will get sick. (*No problem since our backyard is mostly made of brown weeds with hardly any grass.*)

3. Shetlands should be fed hay but grains must be limited as they will make them fat. (*No problem since Dirt was already fat and I didn't know where to get grain.*)

4. Shetlands need clean bedding at all times and it should be changed once or twice a day. Bedding can be straw. (*No problem since there was always plenty of straw and hay in Enid's barn, and I was sure she wouldn't miss a few bales here and there.*)

Humph, I thought, putting down the book for a while and staring at the wall. This didn't seem so hard. Definitely doable. I opened the book again to review a list of other supplies I would need. It looked as though I'd have to get my hands on a shovel, wheelbarrow, and giant tub for water. I also learned that it was possible to teach a pony to pee and poop on command outside with consistent training. Not that there was any choice in the matter. Even I wasn't up for cleaning up after Dirt in the bedroom. Gross.

When I finished with the Muet book, I headed for the

library computer. Luckily, there wasn't the usual crowd of computer geeks waiting in line and I hopped right on without skipping a beat.

Of course, it's important not to believe everything you read online. Once I found a site that advertised the sale of talking cockroaches. Another time, when trying to finish work for school, a picture of a woman with three actual heads popped up. You never really know who's posting things on the Internet, so I've learned to proceed with caution. After all, it's a bit distracting to see multiple heads and talking cockroaches when you're trying to learn stuff about the ancient Greeks or Shetland ponies.

I was happy, however, that my online Shetland research appeared to be on the level. I read about a family in Rhode Island that kept two ponies in the house. There were real videos of the whole family watching television together, the ponies' heads perched over the couch. I also confirmed that it was indeed possible to house-train a Shetland and that this family even enjoyed outings with one of the ponies, seating him right in the backseat with the kids. The other pony stayed at home because he was prone to car sickness.

In Canada, an elderly couple kept their Shetland in the house for years, turning an old wooden chair upside down for a hay trough. Their pony learned to drink from the bathroom-sink tap.

A pediatrician in Ireland housed his pony in the kitchen, where the animal was taught to use a tree stump for a step stool in order to help himself to cookies in the pantry. And another family in Oklahoma kept three (count 'em—three!) Shetlands in the house but drew the line at a fourth.

I also learned that in the seventeenth century, ponies were a sign of wealth among European royalty, some kings and queens making homes for them right in the palaces. And there are Shetlands today trained to be service animals, pulling wheelchairs and guiding the blind.

Well, I thought, exhausted from my studies, *it certainly seemed possible for Dirt to move in, even if it might only be for a short while. Perhaps*, I mused, turning off the computer and reaching for my khaki jacket, *perhaps for a few weeks, a month, or maybe even a year.*

Dirt Moves In

I was completely prepared before Dirt actually moved into the house that Sunday. And it couldn't come soon enough. Images of the horsemeat sign had popped up in my mind ever since I saw it, and the idea that this might be my pony's fate tortured me.

As expected, Enid didn't seem to notice that I borrowed a few bales of hay and straw, and who needed a wheelbarrow anyway when there was a perfectly good cart from the Stop & Shop that had been stuck in the snow all last winter up by Mutter Street? And speaking of the snow, my father kept a sturdy shovel behind the house for winter storms, along with a huge plastic tub crammed with old cans of paint. Perfect for Dirt's water.

Although I was impressed with the Canadian couple's online account of making a kitchen chair into a fashionable hay trough, I didn't have an extra piece of furniture on hand and ended up loading the hay right onto the bedroom floor. Considering Dirt's carefree habits concerning cleanliness, I didn't think he'd mind.

Early that afternoon, my father helped me spread layers and layers of straw bedding on the old wood floor without asking one single question. When I filled up the plastic tub with cold water and carried it inside, he cleared his throat. He traced a wide, wavering step toward me, and took my face in his chapped hand. I could see that the salt in his hair was overcoming the pepper and the creases in his face were deepening. Then he smiled. My father's smiles meant many things at different times, but this time, I knew that he understood. He understood that I needed to rescue Dirt.

When I was just four or five, I remember fishing with my father at Shelter pond. He pulled up a quivering flash of silver and placed it on the pebbles next to me. The fish jumped and shuddered and I dissolved into tears, heartbroken to see something in so much distress. But my gentle father immediately unhooked the fish and threw it back into the lake, taking me in his arms. And so I knew he understood what rescuing meant.

My father wasn't there when Dirt actually moved in, so I handled the big event all on my own. In order to ensure that my pony stayed safely in my yard all day, I had to make certain that it was fully equipped with rotted pumpkins, squashes, and bumpy gourds of all kinds to keep Dirt's interest. Not too difficult to do, seeing as it was such an early fall—pumpkin, squash, and gourd season.

Perfect.

I went up to Dirt and kissed his nose. Mashed squash isn't my favorite food, so I may have wiped off my mouth quickly. Dirt raised his chubby lips in his usual grin, showing off stained, square teeth. I laughed, then attached a piece of old clothesline rope to his worn bridle. He looked up and batted his one eye, already suspicious of what was to come.

But when I tapped him twice on the nose, the command to "walk on," to my surprise, he obeyed promptly. The Muet library book mentioned that Shetlands like to know what's expected of them, and I made a mental note to be as clear as possible from that day forward.

The clothesline in my hand was loose. I didn't even have to pull on it one bit. And so Dirt and I walked slowly into my house, his new home. One step, one hoof, at a time.

My first mistake was storing the hay in a corner of his bedroom. Once Dirt noticed the tempting pile, he shook his head, spun around twice, and lunged. If I hadn't intervened by promptly pulling on the clothesline and then his tail, heavens knows what would have happened. Ms. Muet's book on Shetlands definitely warned about overfeeding.

My second mistake was not realizing how often ponies pee. This first day must have been a record because every time I turned around Dirt was drizzling. The Muet book had also warned that it was harmful for ponies to breathe in their own urine since it was full of ammonia and could hurt their lungs. Each time Dirt peed, I had to make sure that I covered the spot with fresh straw. It seemed that I would have to devote myself to teaching Dirt how to pee and poop on command outside if I didn't want to be constantly shoveling out his room and lugging in more and more new straw.

Taking care of Dirt wasn't going to be easy.

And so we began living together, my father, Dirt, and me; it was certainly an unusual arrangement, but there was really no alternative, considering the circumstances. Early mornings, I'd slip out of my sleeping bag on the kitchen floor, throw on my mother's old khaki jacket and a pair of my father's work boots, and stumble out the back door. First I'd load the shopping cart with just the right amount of hay from where I safely stored it out back under the roof overhang, wheel it into the house, and open Dirt's door to greet him gently. Dirt appreciated a restrained rousing, as he preferred to wake slowly, one limb at a time, until he was finally on his feet. Then, snorting indelicately, he'd gobble up the hay as if he'd been starving. Dirt was most definitely greedy, particularly when faced with food.

I learned not to expect polite morning greetings. In fact, I learned not to expect politeness in any form at all.

Once, Dirt helped himself to some water from the plastic tub outside and sprayed me from head to toe; no question that this was a deliberate crime. Once he shoved me with his head when I was bent over in poop retrieval. Again, he most certainly knew what he was doing. You can't kid a kidder.

But then there was the best part, when Dirt would steady himself, then rest his bulky head right on my shoulder. It was different from when he'd playfully nip, and it was different from when he'd prod me for a treat. First thing in the evening, just before going outside for his nightly walk, Dirt always found the exact right spot on my shoulder to lay down his head, and I'd feel the warmth of its weight all the way through.

Funny how his heavy head on my shoulder always made me feel lighter. Sometimes, the weight of a friend who needs you can lessen your load.

Not that those moments of affection lasted for more than a minute. Soon Dirt and I were tromping together outside and I was giving him the prompt to pee. My raised hand meant "pee," my closed fist meant "poop," and my two hands clapping together meant "quit that messing around and do your business." Well, I can tell you, teaching a pony to relieve himself on cue isn't easy. We'd practice all the time, and still Dirt would pee and poop inside. Then I'd have to haul out the shopping cart all over again, fill it with clean straw, shovel out dirty stuff from Dirt's room, and lay down a brand-new straw bed.

And then there was making sure his water tub was always filled, giving him just the right amount of hay and only a bit of grass outside, brushing him with an old steel brush I found at Shelter Goodwill, and taking him for exercise walks without anyone seeing and wondering. After all, Dirt had been kidnapped and technically could be considered a hostage.

So Dirt and I carried on by ourselves, trotting in and out of the little crooked house, sometimes playing hide-and-seek in our small backyard, sometimes chasing each other in circles or sharing a tidbit of carrot or apple. Every once in a while, I'd imagine a shadow lurking in the cluster of evergreens beyond, someone spying on me, or maybe Enid herself, planning to have me taken away by the police, but I quickly realized guilt was playing tricks with my head. I had reason to feel guilty, having just committed a crime. Although hiding Dirt was just a temporary measure, I was still a thief.

My guilt was only a flash in the pan, however, and I continued to work tirelessly on teaching Dirt my silent commands, and if I was lucky he'd pay attention for a few minutes, but often, he'd balk. In the evenings, we'd stare together at the starry Shelter sky in exhaustion, leaning flank to shoulder, shoulder to flank.

But what I knew and didn't want to think about was how those peaceful days with Dirt might be numbered. Funny how you can put things out of your mind when you want to. Not so funny when there are officials of the state scheming behind your back.

Enough Is Enough

It was the last Friday in September when I finally had enough of Robert Frost Middle School.

Things had been going pretty well through most of the month, and Heywood Prune appeared to have changed most of his evil ways, sometimes leering at me in the hallways but pretty much leaving me alone.

There seemed to be a logical explanation for this. One morning in math class, I overheard Lavinia T. Stout telling Ethan Diggs that Mr. Prune had warned Heywood that if he didn't shape up, he'd be sorry. Even though it really wasn't any of my business, I couldn't help being just a mite pleased that my personal torturer was being kept on a short leash.

So I wasn't prepared for what happened.

The hallways and classrooms were particularly stifling

that morning; I was always surprised when the cool fall was interrupted by a few warm days, steamy weather that frizzed up my hair up so it was as wide as it was tall. And Dirt was particularly lazy on warm days, preferring to nap instead of getting his much-needed exercise.

But I was proud of myself for making it through the entire September at school without any trouble, having successfully ignored anyone who gave me guff, simply trotting by them at a clipped pace when they called me names or tried to trip me outside of class. Those creeps could try all they liked to get under my skin, but I had a wonderful secret, something that they could never imagine or understand.

On that particular Friday, however, something happened that took me entirely by surprise. Despite myself, I was just a little excited since it was the preview day for Book Week, an event that happened only once a year. Although I didn't have money to buy an actual book, I could spend my whole language arts period in the gym, running my hands over the bright covers and skimming as many pages as possible. Maybe Prune would be absent. Maybe he would be sent to study hall for the whole day. Even if he was there, he didn't seem particularly eager to mess with me the way he'd always done before.

My father had agreed to keep Dirt company that day, since I might be home late. Since my father was groggy and somewhat undependable, I reminded him of his promise by wiping his face with cold water first thing in the morning and pulling the blankets off the bed.

"I promise, darlin', that you can count on me," he assured me, drying his face with a corner of the sheet. "You get on going and leave the pony to me. I'll even give him a good brushing the way I've seen you do."

I smiled. Grooming Dirt with the old steel brush always gave both me and my pony pleasure. This early-morning activity seemed to calm us both down, each stroke brushing away any worries or fears. It made me happy to think of my father and Dirt sharing such a pleasant time together in my absence.

Language arts went pretty quickly, and Ms. Wang brought all of us sesame (peanut-free) cookies from home. I thought that was pretty considerate, and ate one quickly and squirreled away the other for later. And Prune was on remarkably good behavior, even standing behind me when we recited the national anthem without pulling my hair or pinching or kicking one bit. By the time the class went downstairs to the gym for the Book Week showcase, I was feeling pretty relaxed. Maybe fifth grade wasn't going to be so bad after all.

My class walked single file down the hallway toward the gym, each student carrying a list of books to buy at the Book Week exhibit set up by our school librarian, Mr. Thomas. Almost everyone except for me had crumpled dollar bills squeezed into damp hands for the purchase of glorious merchandise laid out in the gym on long tables hauled in from the cafeteria.

Lavinia T. Stout was walking right behind me. I could feel her stupid Hello Kitty purse swing against my back.

Lavinia's family owned Stout Handmade Candies downtown, and Lavinia usually had some smear of melting delectable chocolate in her lunch bag. She wore filmy pastel sweaters with brand-new jeans most school days, her shiny blond hair swirled off her face to one side by a Hello Kitty plastic barrette. She also recently started carrying a Hello Kitty patent-leather purse that hung over her shoulder with a gold-link chain. Need I say more?

"Whatcha going to buy, Yonder?" Lavinia mewed sweetly into my ear as the class stopped in front of the gym while Ms. Wang impatiently waved her index finger in the air, hoping beyond hope that would keep us in line. Lavinia preferred to be covered head to toe in pastel yellow on Wednesdays, kind of like she was drowning in pollen.

I shrugged.

"Gonna buy the hair braid book that comes with its own ribbons inside?"

I started to walk faster. Anyone who knows anything about books understands that hair braid books are toys and not worth a hoot.

"Hey, Yonder." I heard Lavinia's new pink sneakers squeaking quickly behind me. "I got some extra money from my pops this morning, but it's just for books. Wanna help me pick something out?"

I admit to being somewhat taken aback. It wasn't as if Lavinia T. Stout usually spoke to me at all, no less asked me to help her. I turned around. Lavinia's bright-yellow profile made my eyes tear.

"Oh, Ms. Wang." Lavinia raised her dimpled hand and smiled ear to ear. "Would it be okay if Yonder helped me pick out some books? I'd be happy to be the class monitor while you speak to Mr. Thomas about the Thanksgiving Feast."

Everyone knew that Ms. Wang had a huge crush on ole Thomas and his dumb plaid too-short-at-the-wrists jacket and protruding belly. And everybody also knew that Mr. Thomas loved to boast about his disgusting gluten-free pumpkin pie that he brought to the school feast every year. Thanksgiving Feast would be our next school event, and many of the teachers brought in delectable homemade treats. Personally, I'm quite fond of gluten, but the thought of any pie, disgusting or not, made my mouth water. Anything other than apples sounded pretty darn good.

"Why, certainly, Lavinia." Ms. Wang's face flushed and her eyelashes actually fluttered like she was having some kind of double pink-eye attack. "That would be very helpful, Yonder."

And before I knew it, Wang and Tubby Thomas were deep in conversation in the back left corner of the gym by the water fountain while Lavinia gripped me by the elbow with a surprisingly firm hand.

Lavinia led me all the way over to the opposite side of the gym, where the poetry books were stacked in uneven piles. I felt my heart thump; these were my very favorite Book Week treasures and, as I peered ahead, Lavinia and I both picking up the pace, I noticed that there wasn't a single person, child or adult, jamming up the table. Apparently, poetry wasn't the first choice of Robert Frost Middle School students.

Lavinia quickly deposited me by the far end of the poetry exhibit, smack in front of a collection of Shel Silverstein anthologies, but as I reached out for one, I felt her push me hard. Real hard. And then again. I whirled around, perfectly prepared to shove her right back, when I came face-to-face with Prune and his gang of puny criminals, who mysteriously appeared out of the adjacent boys' bathroom.

They surrounded me in a semicircle, grinning and chortling like noisy gremlins. I noticed Prune licking his disgusting corn-chip lips and that his usually pale face was puffed up pink. A few red pistachio nuts dropped from his pocket to the floor.

"Well, hello there, Yonder." He smirked. "Fancy meeting you here."

The semicircle moved in closer and closer. One final push and I saw the bathroom door swing open in front of me, and Prune himself put his hands on each side of my waist and pushed with surprising force for such a pipsqueak.

Before I knew what was what, I found myself right in the middle of the boys' bathroom with seven ugly little monsters pointing their grubby fingers right at my face.

"Who's fonder of Yonder?" they chanted. "No one! No one's fonder of Yonder!"

The hair on the back of my neck stood up. This did not bode well.

I opened my mouth in protest.

Prune stepped forward. As usual, he was wearing his brown corduroy pants pulled up high to his chest with his stupid red cowboy belt. He took a quick breath, and before I could raise my hands, Heywood Prune grabbed me roughly. Then, with all his scrawny strength, he rammed his fist into my stomach, sending me gasping to my knees.

"Try to talk now, you dumb mute!" someone yelled as I heaved and flailed. Even in my moment of distress, I made a mental note that "dumb" and "mute" can mean the same thing. Soon the whole stupid mini-mob was chanting, "Yonder, Yonder! Who's fonder of Yonder?"

And that was that. The boys left. I sat there for a minute, trying not to inhale the reek of urine and wet paper towels. If I'd had my wits about me, I might have been interested to see what the boys' bathroom actually looked like; after all, I had never been in one before. But things being as they were, I slowly, very slowly, got to my feet, noticing that my fingers trembled, and stumbled back into the gym. For a minute, I thought I might throw up on the shiny blue-and-white floor.

All activity in the gym continued as it had before. No one was at the poetry table. Ms. Wang and Mr. Thomas were still in the far corner, heads bent in eager conversation. The kids continued to stare at books, bright-green bills pressed in their hands. Nobody looked up. Prune and his gang seemed to have disappeared, although as I turned to the gym's double glass doors, I saw them giggling together at the science-book table like stupid gossiping girls.

I took a deep breath. I opened one gym door and then the other. I walked down the lower level hallway, then up the stairs to my locker, where I grabbed my mother's soft khaki jacket. And then I marched all the way through the middle school corridor, past the bulletin board drawings of mythological creatures from ancient Greece that we had made earlier that fall. Pegasus was mine, and I ripped it from the wall, then crumpled it quickly with one hand. As I strode straight out the Robert Frost Middle School front door, I tossed the paper ball backward without even turning around to see where it landed.

My Secret Is Revealed

I ran all the way home, absolutely, positively done with Robert Frost Middle School forever and ever. Heywood Prune, Ethan Diggs, Lavinia T. Stout, and their gang of criminals weren't going to have me to push around anymore. My mind was made up. There would be no returning to school, Trudy or no Trudy.

To my relief, I found Dirt and my father in the kitchen sharing an apple. Both brightened when they saw me.

"Good day, darlin'?" my father asked absently.

It was eleven a.m. and I had been gone only three hours. He turned to pour himself a large mug of special cider and gave the rest of the apple to Dirt.

I rushed to throw my arms around Dirt and bury my face in his neck.

"Well, this old pony of yours and I did fine," my father

continued. "There might have been a few messes inside when I was napping but I'm planning to clean them up spick-and-span."

I knew that my father did his best. I knew that he wanted to help. But I also knew that Dirt probably hadn't had a single walk in my absence and probably hadn't even had his late-morning snack.

It was okay. Since I wasn't going back to Robert Frost, I wouldn't have to depend on my father to help with Dirt or for anything else. Sometimes, it's just easier not to ask anyone for anything and to take care of things yourself.

Apparently, it was an orchard day, so after finishing his cider, my father gave me a kiss on the head, put on his favorite black baseball cap, and sauntered out the front door. I quickly cleaned up any poop and hay that had been left behind on the floor, gave Dirt a brief walk outside, then settled him back in his room.

By then it was almost noon. Closing Dirt's door behind me, I started to the kitchen to make myself a double-decker apple sandwich with a day-old biscuit from the bakery when who did I hear banging on the front door?

Not again! Not so soon! I froze midbite, my sandwich gripped tightly with both hands. I hadn't even had a full hour to hammer out a new plan.

"Open the door, Yonder. I know that you're in there. And I'm not happy you left school in the middle of the day!"

What to do? It wasn't as though I thought Trudy wasn't going to return; I just hoped it wouldn't be for a while and I'd catch a break. Coming back to spy on me so soon seemed like overkill. I needed some time to take a breath and figure things out, for goodness' sake. No such luck.

The knocking continued.

It seemed that I really didn't have a choice, so slowly, dragging one foot behind the other, I headed to the front door. I wasn't looking forward to hearing what Trudy had to say.

She did not look happy. Her arms were crossed over her chest and she was tapping one foot on the ground. I noted that her red hat was dented and one of her short, stiff braids had unraveled, some stray hairs sticking to her cheek. Her forehead glistened with sweat, and her pink lipstick had mostly worn off, leaving a little leftover neon dot on the corner of one lip.

"It certainly took you enough time to open up," Trudy sputtered, immediately scanning the house. "I thought we had an agreement that you'd get yourself to school every day and *stay* there.

"And now," she continued, brushing past me into the house, "I had to come all the way back here again, and this time your principal called me since you apparently hightailed it out of school without permission and in the middle of the day." She stopped to glare at me for a minute. "I'm going to see what's really what."

Before I could stop her or even catch a breath, Trudy marched into my living room and headed to my father's open bedroom door. I could hardly believe it, but she had the nerve to stick her head all the way inside, call out his name, then turn right around and head for Dirt's room.

"Where is your father, Yonder?" Trudy was dead serious, definitely not messing around. "I'd like to speak with him immediately."

There wasn't any time to intervene. She knocked on the second bedroom door with grim determination and pushed it open, although I tried to block her with an extended leg.

I held my breath and heard a clamor of words spill.

"As I live and breathe!" she exclaimed finally, and then repeated herself: "As I live and breathe!"

Dirt turned around lazily to look at her with his one good eye, as if to assess the situation at hand, a wad of hay in his mouth, and then slowly swung it back around again, clearly more interested in his snack.

"Yonder," Trudy said haltingly, trying to catch her breath, "what in God's name is that creature doing in your house? I may look like a fancy city gal"—she touched her hat with one hand as if for emphasis—"but I grew up in the country, just like you. And just like you"—she hesitated for a moment, and I thought I saw her lip tremble—"I grew up without much guidance. But I never, and I mean never, met anyone who kept a pony in the house! There surely must be sanitation regulations . . . This must be against the law."

I shrugged.

While I wasn't sure I believed in the Almighty, I absolutely knew that it was never proper for adults in authority to use his name so nastily, especially when in the company of impressionable youth.

"How long has the animal been inside?" Dirt's presence in the house was evidently extremely upsetting to Trudy. She bit her lower lip, and her eyes looked wild. "Promise me that you'll get rid of it immediately. I'm guessing you thought it best to keep it out of the rain today and that this is a highly unusual circumstance. But, Yonder"—Trudy stopped to catch a breath—"animals can easily tolerate rain, and you must promise me that you'll take it back to its stable or wherever you have it tied up outside, so I won't have to file a report and formally intervene. I really don't want a formal intervention, as I'm not yet sure that would be the best option for anyone. But you just can't continue like this, doing whatever you feel like no matter what. There are consequences to breaking rules, and it seems as if you're breaking every rule in the book. You're not living on your own island, for heaven's sake."

I nodded just to calm her. I certainly didn't see the need for such hysteria.

From inside the bedroom, I could hear Dirt pressing his head against the door. Of course, I had closed it quickly after observing Trudy's horror and shock; there was certainly no point in overextending their first and evidently traumatic visit.

Whack.

Dirt's head butted the door, then jiggled the doorknob. He was a very curious pony, a quality shared by the Shetland breed. I had read about this in the Muet book.

What to do? Let out Dirt and risk upsetting Trudy even more, or make her a cup of my father's iced apple cider, a brew he concocted every fall?

I looked up at Trudy and she looked back at me.

"It's not as if I think you're a bad girl, Yonder," she finally said quietly. "I know that you've managed to keep up your grades and have been through a lot of sorrow. And it couldn't have been easy. But it just isn't acceptable for a girl of your age not to go to school, and it certainly isn't acceptable to keep a horse inside your house. Does your father know about this? Of course, he must. Whether he does or he doesn't, if the horse isn't gone as soon as possible, then I'll have to call the authorities. What were you thinking, and what, for goodness' sake, was your father thinking?"

Pony, not horse, I thought. *Shetland pony from the Shetland Islands.*

By now, Trudy had begun muttering to herself, as if she forgot that I was standing right next to her. It occurred to me that Trudy might not be of sound mind.

But I knew better. I knew she was right, and I knew that I lived in a very peculiar manner. After all, how many eleven-year-old girls locked their fathers into bedrooms at night and slept on the kitchen floor so their pet Shetland pony could have a bedroom all to himself? How many girls had no one to tell them what to eat or what to wear? To go to school or go to sleep or brush their hair or do homework or be careful when talking with someone they didn't know? How many girls chose not to say a single word, to not ever speak, so that they would never have to answer questions about not having a mother? How many eleven-year-old girls lay on the cold floor each and every night, comforted by the sound of a three-hundred-pound pony's breath as it thundered through the long, lonely night?

I handed Trudy a glass of my father's special cider. I watched Trudy gulp it down and grimace. Her eyes flew open wide.

"Why, this isn't cider at all, Yonder, you little scamp. This is moonshine you've given me!" But she puckered up and took another long sip, smacking her lips afterward, then pushed the cup quickly away as if it were contaminated. "Now let's see that animal of yours again," she finally sputtered, squaring her shoulders as if about to face an enemy of some kind. "I want to be sure I know what I saw, and it looked to me as though what I saw was trouble."

And so Trudy and I walked back to the second bedroom door and stood in front of it for a moment, so close that our arms were almost touching. As if on cue, as if someone had counted from one to three, we pushed open the door together.

Dirt was waiting for us. And the minute he saw Trudy, I swear that for the first and last time, I heard my pony actually chuckle. The sound was a cross between chalk on a blackboard and a deep-throated bellow. Both high and low at the same time. Dirt rolled back his lips and grinned a yellow-toothed pony smile. And then he reached directly over my head to merrily fling Trudy's hat right up into the air.

It seemed to hover by the ceiling for a moment, then spiraled downward, spinning directly onto the only head in the room with a yellow forelock and two downy, pointed pony ears.

It was long-lost love after that. Dirt had found another human to call his own. In that single moment, Trudy the Terrible was terrible no more. She bowed her head and then exploded in a belly laugh.

But betrayal was slowly brewing.

Believe it.

Trudy the Traitor

Although Trudy had been briefly amused by Dirt's charming ways, I knew that she would continue to check up on me after the weekend to make sure I'd moved my pony out of the house and that I'd returned to school. But the weather was so nice, clear and sunny, and Dirt and I passed the weekend so pleasantly, taking short walks, practicing commands and generally enjoying each other's company, that I chose not to worry. By Monday, I'd put Trudy out of my mind. I should have been frightened. I should have known what was to come. But I preferred living in a state of disbelief, hoping beyond hope that my worst fears would never come to pass.

Late the following day, I was minding my own business, making Dirt a snack of apples and oatmeal. While I knew that Ms. Muet would not approve of Dirt eating too many grains, I thought it was okay every once in a while. Everyone needs a special treat, after all.

Dirt was waiting quietly behind me on his best behavior until I heard him neigh.

Not good.

"Yonder?"

I couldn't believe my ears. Trudy was back and I wasn't going to get a single break. This wasn't going to be good.

The oatmeal in the pot in front of me was just about to boil and if it overcooked, it might start to be sort of slimy. Dirt hated slimy oatmeal.

"Yonder! Please open up."

Good gracious. Get a grip.

As the perfectly polite person that I am and minding my manners, I stopped stirring to think about letting Trudy, soon to be Trudy the Traitor, into my house all over again. Maybe if I didn't answer her, she'd give up and go away.

I couldn't help but wonder how this woman managed to get anything done, considering all the time she was spending at my house.

"Yonder!"

I sighed, and Dirt suddenly nosed the wooden spoon lying on the stove.

Quit it! I managed to pry the utensil from his mouth.

It was clear that Trudy wasn't leaving and that I'd better answer before she made a scene.

I didn't bother faking a welcoming smile or inviting Trudy inside. What did it matter, anyway? She was an official social worker and could do as she wanted, unlike an eleven-year-old girl who didn't talk.

Dirt, however, was an entirely different story.

The minute he glimpsed Trudy at the front door, Dirt swung his head over my shoulder, rolled back his lips, and lunged cheerfully toward our visitor.

For a moment, Trudy froze, then shot me an aggravated look.

"Get that thing you call a horse offa me."

Another instance of poor manners, I thought as I calmly pulled on Dirt's thick mane. He backed up for a moment, loosening his grip. Then he changed his mind again, pushing past me.

This wasn't going to be good.

In a blink of an eye, Dirt had his nose in Trudy's shirt pockets. My guess was that she had something tempting stowed inside.

"Back!" Trudy moaned. "Back, you disgusting beast."

I thought it was rude for Trudy to call Dirt disgusting, and he was also particularly sensitive to the word *beast* considering his history with Enid. I took a deep breath so as not to lose my temper. But the truth was, I was furious at them both: Trudy for calling Dirt names, and Dirt for misbehaving so fiendishly. I tried not to think about how pleasant Trudy had been when we first met, how she listened when I didn't speak and how she was patient when I pretended not to hear.

Dirt pushed me again and nibbled at my ear.

Enough.

I was exhausted.

Stop.

I looked sternly at Dirt and rapped him on the rump. As usual, he understood my command and immediately stilled.

Good boy.

He backed up again, crushing a book I had left on the floor, and then chewed on it nervously, nearly knocking over a nearby lamp.

Careful.

Dirt looked up at me, his one eye blinking furiously. That always meant the same thing: He was ravenous. But it was too late to lure him inside the bedroom again, so I just watched as he headed for the oatmeal, devouring it straight from the pan.

Drat. I had really hoped to save some for his breakfast.

Poor Trudy stood up slowly and glared at me. A scrap from her polka-dot hat stuck to one pant leg, and the other remnants had blown off the front steps in a sudden gust of wind. She brushed off her knees, then her arms, then her face. I could see that I had my work cut out for me. Trudy was going to be a challenge.

I wanted to explain why I needed to keep Dirt inside the house, although I knew it wasn't typical behavior, and I wanted to explain to her why I was so worried about school. I wanted to tell her about the kids who teased and tortured me. I wanted to explain how hard I worked to keep my grades up. That I read my books and did my homework at the worn kitchen table each and every night, no matter that my father was locked in his bedroom in his own house night after night, sobbing and sobbing, his floor littered with bottles of beer, no matter that I didn't know what to do, how to calm him down, how to help the hurt, no matter how I tried not to listen and to finish my homework anyway, no matter that my writing was blurred by tears.

No matter what.

I wanted to tell Trudy that there was no choice but to keep Dirt out of sight and inside the house, that there was no choice at all, that horrid Enid would pack him off on the factory truck, that she would soon send him to the slaughterhouse and get a bundle of crisp dollar bills in return.

I wanted to tell her how Dirt learned to listen to me when I didn't speak a word.

I wanted to tell her all of it. Everything.

My throat throbbed and my mouth chattered.

But it was too late.

Too late for Trudy, too late for Dirt, and too late for me.

Before I turned around to face Trudy again, she had

already started down the path away from our house, her round shoulders thrown back. A river of pony slobber trailed from her right shoulder all the way down to her ample rear.

Wait, I wanted to call.

Stop, I started to say.

But *wait* and *stop* were just words in my own head and only Dirt could hear me. Only Dirt really ever heard or understood.

The Authorities Arrive

"Anyone home?"

I was sitting at the kitchen table, just one day after Trudy's last unfortunate visit, carefully counting my newest collection of tarnished coins found in the backyard pond. If I just collected one dollar more, I could buy two cheese biscuits at the town bakery. But the knocking broke my concentration.

A visitor was the last thing I needed at the moment, and I turned to listen carefully.

"Anyone home?"

It certainly didn't sound like Trudy.

I quickly eyed the door to Dirt's room. Thank goodness, it was safely shut and all seemed quiet from inside.

Was it my imagination or did I hear the front door creak open? Nobody could be that rude. Who would possibly let themselves into my very own house? Unless it was a robber or ax murderer of some kind. Hiding my newfound wealth, I slipped the coins into my pocket and bolted to my feet. I didn't have a chance to look around for a weapon because a tall man in a gray suit marched himself right into the kitchen. I could hardly believe my eyes.

His white hair was buzzed short to the scalp and his maroon striped tie was held by some kind of bent clip. He didn't look like a criminal to me and yet you never know. And then I saw a woman trotting directly behind. Both intruders had white plastic badges hung around their necks as if they were volunteering at the Robert Frost book fair.

"You must be Yonder." The tall man smiled. He had a surprisingly soft voice.

I crossed my arms. My expression must have been one of horror.

"It's okay, dear." The woman reached for my hand and I stepped back quickly. "No need to be afraid. The door was open and when nobody answered—"

But I *was* afraid. My stomach had immediately squeezed itself into a hard ball. I couldn't believe that what was happening was real.

"We're from Child and Family Services," the man interrupted. "We work with Trudy. Trudy Trumpet. And we've had the most disturbing report. Something about your missing school and keeping a large animal—a horse—in the house. That certainly couldn't be, could it?"

A pox on that Trudy! I could hardly believe my ears or imagine that she would have the heart to actually turn me in. Apparently, I was dead wrong.

Both the man and woman pointed to their badges as if to say, *See. We're official. Don't worry your pretty little head.*

I couldn't be fooled by any dumb badges and had a cold, sinking feeling of what was to come. But at least my pony was safe behind closed doors.

"Sweetheart," the woman said slowly. Clearly, she didn't realize that my hearing was intact. "Do you mind if we sit down? Now, it's certainly evident that the ludicrous report was incorrect, and we don't see any horses roaming around."

The man and woman exchanged smiles and then sighed in relief.

I shook my head. No one but me was going to sit down if I had it my way.

Neither the man nor the woman seemed to care what I wanted or didn't want. Both just turned to me again and stared. I noticed that the woman was dressed in tweed from head to toe and was wearing a crisp, white button-down shirt under her jacket.

They plopped themselves right down at the kitchen table without hesitation, despite my clear instruction otherwise.

I remained standing. My faced burned with fear and shame.

"I know that this is difficult," the man said quietly. The left-hand side of his bottom lip twitched.

"And we're sorry to bring up painful subjects." The woman had a small brown stain on one corner of her white shirt cuff. Chocolate? Despite myself, my mouth started to water. "It's dreadful to lose a mother at your age. And of course we sympathize, but it's been a number of years now and you simply must attend school regularly."

Anger whipped through me so fast that I thought I might fall backward. Who did this stranger think she was to mention my mother to me? I didn't want her sympathy or anything else.

"Yes," the man said. "Yes. And there's another matter as well. But we do need to speak with your father right away. It's imperative."

I knew what *imperative* meant. This was going to be bad. Very bad.

"Is your father home, dear?" The woman's mouth looked gooey with dark lipstick.

I shook my head.

They both squinted at me as if they had never seen a girl before, sighed together, and stood up.

"Do you mind if we look around?" The man's voice was firm, not exactly kind anymore.

I nodded. I did mind. And yet the two determined intruders continued to ignore me, walking themselves out of the kitchen, through the living room, and directly toward my father's bedroom.

My father's door was ajar and they peered inside, first one and then the other.

It was hard to imagine that anybody could be so impolite.

The woman closed the door carefully. "Tsk, tsk," she said. "Tsk, tsk."

The man was scribbling quickly on a long yellow pad. "Did you see the bottles?" he asked the woman. "And the room reeks of you-know-what."

She nodded. "The beer cans as well. Littered all over the floor. Oh my."

Had they forgotten that I was still standing right there? Extremely rude to talk to each other about my father without acknowledging my presence. Despite myself, my hands began to shake.

"We're just going to look around a bit more, dear. We'll be out of your hair soon."

Clearly, no one was even asking for my permission anymore.

The man looked quickly through the kitchen, having the nerve to open our lopsided cabinet and the refrigerator too. The woman dusted the table with her index finger and then looked at it disapprovingly. But when they both turned to Dirt's room, I froze.

The woman looked up at me and grinned. "I see this room is private."

They were both chuckling at the paper sign I had taped to Dirt's door: DANGER. NO ONE ALLOWED.

I didn't think that the situation called for humor of any

kind. My heart fluttered, then broke out into a full-on gallop. I could hardly breathe.

"This must be your room," the man said. "Mind if we take a quick peek?"

I shook my head vehemently, knowing in my heart of hearts that it wouldn't make a difference and that they'd let themselves right inside whether I agreed or not. But I flung myself against the door anyway. You never know when a good flinging can stop someone in their tracks.

The woman sighed and the man simply reached right over my head. Just like that. Just like I wasn't even there. He pushed, and I shuddered.

Dirt's door swung open easily. I took a deep breath.

Friendly pony that he was, Dirt was pleased to have visitors. He startled when he first noticed the strangers, then stomped one hoof in a welcoming sign. I couldn't help but be a bit proud of his excellent manners.

The woman gasped.

The man took her elbow in a gesture I thought to be protective, but then I realized he had pushed her in front of him like a shield. Embarrassing, to say the least.

"But I didn't think, we didn't believe . . . When Ms. Trumpet told us, we thought . . . It was impossible to believe that a horse was living . . . impossible to think . . ."

I ran over to Dirt's side, grabbed him by the mane, and tapped him twice on his nose. This was the signal to walk.

Walk on, I said to my pony silently. *Walk on, Dirt, please walk on.*

He just turned to me with the goofiest of expressions, a few straws of hay stuck in his mouth, then spun around again to gaze at the man and woman. My heart stopped.

Then, pleased as he could be, just as if he was trying to show off, Dirt plopped out the largest turd he had ever managed during his time living with me. It stunk to high heaven.

The woman retched, and as if he was in on a joke, Dirt responded with his magnificent smile, rolling back his lips and showing his massive yellow teeth. His ears pricked up with clear interest.

"It's going to bite me!" The woman waved her hands in front of Dirt, which I knew to be a terrible mistake. The waving of hands was a signal I had established for Dirt to approach quickly.

Still showing his teeth and letting out a peevish bray, my pony headed for the woman, his head shaking back and forth.

"Call 9-1-1!" the man yelled to the woman. "Call animal control. Go!"

The woman slid out of his grasp and ran to the kitchen. The man backed up slowly. You'd think he was encountering some kind of predator in the wild.

WALK ON, DIRT. I grabbed his mane and pulled him

toward me, and to my relief he turned right around, glancing back every once in a while at the two strangers scrambling for safety.

I knew what was coming. Terror raced through my entire body and my teeth were chattering. Animal control would take away my pony if they captured him. He'd go back to Enid. Back to being horsemeat for sale.

When we reached the front door, I tapped Dirt's nose four times, a command calling for him to pick up the speed, and then pulled his mane with all my might. Dirt neighed happily, agreeably trotting ahead as if for his daily walk.

My face, arms, and hands were cold, numb with fear.

Once we made it safely outside, Dirt quickly settled himself by the front path, nibbling the brown weeds. I knew I was in trouble then. It was impossible to get Dirt to obey when eating.

The man and woman were still hollering orders to each other from inside. I could hear their voices echo through the open doorway and knew that I didn't have much time.

Go, Dirt! I yelled silently. *Go. Walk on, walk on, walk on.*

He continued to ignore my commands and to chew the weeds merrily. I made my final move.

Go, Dirt! I whacked his rump, but he didn't budge.

I imagined police sirens blaring from down Mutter Street.

And then I remembered the hose. The green garden hose

hanging right outside the front door. I knew I would hate myself later, and yet I also knew I had no choice.

Grabbing the garden hose with both hands, I waved it over my head.

My heart in my mouth, I threw the hose in the air and watched it land by my pony's feet. His whole body shuddered. He looked up plaintively at me, as if asking for help.

Tears sprang to my eyes. I wasn't crying, and then I was.

I shook the hose on the ground and slid it toward him, watching as he backed away, one quivering step at a time.

Go. Walk on. Hurry.

If there was ever a time I wanted to speak, it was then.

Run away, Dirt, I would have screamed. *Run as fast as you can.*

I opened my mouth and couldn't even call his name.

Hurry. Walk on right now.

Last chance, Dirt; last chance, buddy. My whole face was wet with tears by now. I waved the hose again, brandishing it over my head like a sword. It felt slimy in my hands.

Dirt's one eye rolled back in his head and he skittered from side to side.

Go.

And so he did. He took one last look at me, then lumbered around so that all I could see between the house and the road was my pony's broad butt. I heard him snort and sputter.

Dirt cantered clumsily away, faster than I had ever seen

him move, away from my little crooked house and away from my life. I squeezed my eyes shut and wished as hard as I had ever wished for anything in my whole entire life. I wished for to Dirt to keep moving forward past anyone or anything that would do him harm, past the long arm of the authorities and past Enid's farm. I wished for him to run away and to not turn back.

I wished so hard that I couldn't move.

The man and the woman were waiting for me when I turned around. I knew that they would be taking me away that very day. I knew that I had no choice but to go with them and that my father would come home to find me gone. I wanted to ask if I could leave him a note saying good-bye, but, of course, asking wasn't a possibility. So I just stood there, frozen, as they told me that it was time to go.

In those few minutes, I was no longer Yonder. I had become a girl without a home and who had just lost her only friend.

A fork in the road, Yonder, my father had once said. Which way will you choose to go?

PART TWO

Foster Care

I woke up the next morning with no idea where I was. Why wasn't I sleeping in my own torn sleeping bag on my own kitchen floor, and where were my father and Dirt? I looked around the unfamiliar pink room with pink-and-white-flowered curtains and swallowed. Maybe I was dreaming, and then maybe turned into:

Oh no.

The evening before slowly began to return. I crushed my face into my pillow and tried not to think, to remember. But I did remember.

I remembered the authorities.

I remembered my corduroy pants and denim overalls stuffed into a brown paper bag.

I remembered being dragged out of the house. I remembered kicking.

I remembered a drive in a long, strange car and that it was getting dark outside.

I remembered sobbing and sobbing without making a sound and finally dropping off to sleep on the shoulder of someone I didn't even know.

I remembered driving Dirt away with the hose and putting him in danger of becoming horsemeat.

I rubbed my eyes and slid up in bed, then looked around the bedroom. A small painting of a golden horse in a silver frame glittered next to one window. My heart stopped. On the other side of the room hung a large mirror that faced a wall and reflected nothing but blank pink. I made a decision to never stand in front of that mirror and look at my own unfamiliar self. There would be nothing to recognize.

The corners of my eyes were sticky from crying.

It had been a long night without much sleep and I had tossed and turned in a too-soft bed that made me feel as though I were sinking underwater all the way down to the ocean's floor.

I had dreamt that my father was sinking with me, and I dreamt about Dirt. My pony had wings in my dream and was flying above me in an apple-cider sky. He opened his pony mouth but only silence puffed out in a cloud. And then the cloud turned into letters that turned into words. When I tried to read them, each word dropped from the sky and shattered on the ground.

I may have lost Dirt forever.

I blew my nose with a tissue from a flowered box next to the bed, then wiped my nose all over again with my sleeve. To my surprise, I discovered that I was wearing a white flannel nightgown with a ruffled neck. I didn't recognize the itchy puffy thing and couldn't remember putting it on.

"Everything all right in there, dear?" I heard a woman's nasal voice from the other side of the door. "It's Mrs. Prattle, your new foster mother, and we're looking forward to having you join us for breakfast."

Prattle? What kind of name was that? And who was "we"?

I pulled the top bedsheet up to my chin. It was very soft and very pink.

The door creaked open slowly. A head poked in and then poked out. The door closed again and someone knocked.

"Okay if I come in, dear?"

Did the woman expect me to actually answer? Hadn't the authorities given her any information about the stranger sleeping in her pink bed?

I stretched the sheet over my head and scooted down under the blankets. I was terrified; I was angry; I didn't even know exactly where this dumb foster house was. What if I had been sent to another state? Wasn't transporting a minor over state lines a crime?

Silence, then: "We'll be downstairs in the kitchen when you're ready, dear."

The foster mother's name actually was Prattle and the foster father said to just call him Pa. They introduced themselves at the kitchen table when I finally made my way slowly downstairs.

I thought they looked too old to be parents, foster or otherwise. Their hair was gray, for goodness' sake. Even their eyebrows.

Most definitely too old and too stuffy to ever keep a pony in their too-clean house.

"Would you like your eggs scrambled or over easy, dear?" Mrs. Prattle asked, wiping her hands on her apron. The bright yellow-and-blue-striped kitchen wallpaper made my eyes burn. "Scrambled or over easy, Yonder, dear?" she repeated.

Again, I wondered why no one bothered to tell her that I didn't speak. It seemed to me that this information might have been important to understand before she agreed to bring me inside her home, eat at her stupid kitchen table, and sleep in her sinkable bed.

And what was the story with the old man? Didn't he have anything to say? I studied his face for a moment, wondering if he had any teeth. Most old men had fake teeth, although I couldn't remember how I knew that.

I crossed my arms. Mr. Prattle didn't look up. He had a stubble of white at the tip of his chin.

"We'll all have scrambled, then." Mrs. Prattle flushed and turned toward the stove. I glared at the floor. "And don't you worry, Yonder, dear, we'll get you back home with your father as soon as possible. I know this must be difficult."

Difficult? The woman didn't know that half of it. But "soon" wasn't going to cut it. If I didn't hurry and scram away from all things Prattle, I might never see my pony again.

But, naturally, I scarfed up my eggs without hesitation. They barely had a minute to quiver on the plate. It was important that I keep up my strength.

Mrs. Prattle was large, tall, and big-boned with strawberry splotches on her cheeks and silver hair caught in a knot at the nape of her neck, while Pa was much smaller. He had wisps of white hair with shiny scalp showing through and he laid his wide-brimmed fedora on the table as he slowly ate his breakfast. I noticed that a wooden cane trembled against his chair.

The Prattles surprised me with their grandparent hair, strawberry splotches, and old-man canes. Weren't foster parents supposed to be lean and mean? I had read stories that often ended with the poor children tied to bedposts or locked in cellars.

"Drink all your milk, Yonder, dear," Mrs. Prattle said to me as she filled an enormous glass. "If you don't drink all your milk, then we won't have healthy bones, will we, dear?"

I didn't see Mrs. Prattle drinking any stupid milk.

Maybe this was just another version of evil foster care. They were going to torture me with syrupy sweetness and tepid milk instead of slapping me around or starving me in chains.

Mrs. Prattle smiled down at me the way Dirt smirked at his prey, the way he looked at Trudy the Traitor during their final, disastrous encounter.

"Now, be sure to take a nice shower, Yonder, dear, but before you do, I want to give you our address and phone number here at the house, just in case you should need them in an emergency of some kind or if you ever get lost. The social workers who brought you here said that I should make sure you know how to find the house in all circumstances, seeing as this is a brand-new home for you. And I thought this was a wonderful idea. They made some other suggestions too, since we're new at foster parenting, but we can talk over those later."

Did the woman ever shut up? And this was certainly not my home.

Mrs. Prattle smiled widely and handed me a slip of paper on which she had carefully printed the address, each number and letter drawn with curlicues. No surprise there.

I was quite good at memorizing, thank you very much, and certainly didn't need any stupid paper.

"Now, time for your shower, dear. And make sure that you wash all over. Even your privates."

I was furious then. I felt my face swell up red and my eyebrows catch on fire. Who in the world did this woman think she was, instructing me on how, when, and where to clean myself? Privates were called just that for a good reason. And I'd already washed my hands before breakfast and thought a shower was taking cleanliness to a ridiculous level.

My stomach felt bloated and I burped loudly. Right there in the Prattles' yellow kitchen.

Pa laughed. Mrs. Prattle held her napkin to her mouth. I didn't feel the least embarrassed and planned on burping much more in the future. Maybe that would rattle Prattle. Maybe that would get me sent home to my father, to my little crooked house, and to Dirt.

I didn't know what frightened me more: being away from my father or losing Dirt to the great beyond. After all, I had no idea where my pony had gone and it was all my fault that he left in the first place. Well, not all my fault. The authorities sure had something to do with it too.

I spent much of the day refusing to leave the foster bedroom, with Mrs. Prattle knocking at the door every two minutes, insisting that I get ready for school.

School? Was she kidding? No chance.

"Mr. Prattle and I have decided it would be okay for you to stay at home today, and social services has agreed," Mrs. Prattle finally said with a heavy sigh from the other side of the door. "I just got off the phone with your social worker. A day of adjustment, dear, but it is important to get a bit of fresh air."

I certainly was going to give her "fresh" if she didn't let up. I stared at the nauseating pink walls closing in on me, at the bedroom door that unfortunately didn't have a lock, and at the two windows with flowered curtains fluttering in the breeze.

Wait.

One of the windows was open a few inches. Scrambling out of bed, I next dashed over to the open window and pushed. Not locked. My heart thumped.

Escape. If I played my cards right, I could make it out of this stupid pink room, sidle down from the window, and somehow find my way to rescue Dirt.

There wasn't any time to waste. If Enid captured Dirt or if he trotted back to her farm after the previous night's green hose incident, it would all be over. I started to shiver at the thought. I wouldn't, couldn't let that happen.

The window was easy to move. I pushed it open, then looked back in the room for my khaki jacket. Darn, it had been left downstairs in the kitchen last night, and I absolutely couldn't leave it behind.

Quickly, I hatched out a plan. I'd slide down the fat vine attached to the clapboard siding outside the window, grab on to the thick branch that would quickly come within reach, shimmy down the tree, scoot around the house, then sneak back in through the kitchen door, where my khaki jacket was hanging on a hook.

It wouldn't be an easy feat to accomplish. The foster bedroom was all the way up on the second floor, not like my first-floor room in the little crooked house, where I could easily climb out the window without incident.

But Dirt needed me. I didn't have a choice.

Nudging myself forward slowly and carefully, I slid one leg over the open windowsill and then the other and looked down. I'd have to be careful. One wrong move and splat, a "Yonder, dear" pancake would land flat on the ground below.

I reached for the vine. It was stuck tightly to the house and seemed as if it might hold my weight for a minute until I could reach for the tree branch.

But as I looked down again, who did I see looking straight up at me? It was Pa, holding a pair of hedge clippers. And then to my horror, I heard Mrs. Prattle screaming right behind me at the top of her lungs.

Prattle grabbed hold of my pants waistband and pulled. My head hit the top of the window. She screamed again and pulled me harder. "Yonder, don't! Please, things will get better, I promise. Come back inside right now. Please!"

Good grief, woman, I thought, *there's no need for a melt-down. Take it down a notch or two.* Did she really think that I was trying to do myself in?

I just sat there on that foster bedroom windowsill, my legs flapping downward and my hands gripping the two sides of the wall with all my might, and wondering how long I could maintain that position. If I slid forward, I'd end up facing Pa and his hedge clippers; if I squirmed backward, I'd have to deal with the hysterical Mrs. Prattle. So I just sat there for a few long minutes, completely flummoxed about what to do.

And *flummoxed* was the perfect word for what I was feeling. Flummoxed, scared, and horribly sad. Caught between two pretend parents who I didn't even know—away from my real home, my real father, and my pony, who was my one real friend—I hovered, not knowing which direction to go. Backward or forward?

A fork in the road, Yonder. Which way?

I closed my eyes then, just for a minute, and inhaled my own scent of sweat and fear. If I hadn't been so determined to ignore Trudy, if I'd done a better job of taking care of my father and at hiding Dirt, if I'd been a better protector of my pony, if I'd only been able to say what I meant and ask for what I needed . . .

I saw a frightened Dirt inside the black of my lids. I saw his one eye fixed on the green hose in terror and then on me in disbelief. A warm tear rolled down my cheek. My pony was roaming lost somewhere, without a friend to his name. Not even his very best friend, who he thought he could count on.

I smelled Dirt's scent instead of mine. I felt his whiskers brushing my palm and his satiny lips nibbling at my cheek, my neck.

Longing wrapped around my chest and squeezed so tightly that I could hardly breathe.

"Please, Yonder, dear, please!" Mrs. Prattle's shrill voice interrupted my thoughts and I startled despite myself.

I shimmied my rump back through the window, scooted around, and calmly dropped down to the bedroom floor. Mrs. Prattle was still screaming and Pa was standing next to her now, trying to settle her with a few awkward pats on the head. This was hard for him to accomplish since he was a good foot shorter than his wife.

I closed the window behind me calmly, smoothed down my pants where they had been so rudely disheveled by grasping foster hands, and marched right back to the foster bed. By then, Mrs. Prattle had stopped screaming, but was still snatching at me and repeating "Oh dear, oh dear, oh dear."

I was a smidgen discouraged that my plan for escape had failed, but I had all night to figure out a new one. No one—Trudy, Mrs. Prattle, or Pa—would keep me away from Dirt.

Stroke

When I locked myself in the foster bathroom the next morning, I just wanted a little bit of privacy for a few minutes of weeping. It was hard being an underwater girl far away from shore, and I was struggling as hard as I could to stay afloat without anyone knowing I was drowning. And I couldn't let myself drown, although that might have been easier—I had to be on alert at all times. Figuring out an escape plan for me and a rescue plan for Dirt wouldn't be easy.

I missed Dirt so much that my throat hurt. I couldn't bear to think about what might happen to him if I didn't do something and do it quick. I usually wasn't much of a crybaby, but I wept and wept in the cramped foster bathroom that morning. And I couldn't seem to stop.

So I wasn't pleased to hear Mrs. Prattle interrupt my

private time with her cloying voice. Wouldn't you know that she'd pick the very worst moment?

"Yonder, dear," Mrs. Prattle called from the other side of the door. "Everything okay in there?"

Everything was not.

"You have a visitor, dear. Someone to see you. Please come downstairs."

Visitor? I took a deep breath. Who in the world could be visiting me? Had my father come to finally bring me home again?

I wiped my nose on my shirtsleeve and flung open the bathroom door, then quickly followed Mrs. Prattle downstairs to the foyer. My heart was racing and I thought I might combust. But when I reached the living room, it wasn't my father waiting for me at all, but a round, short woman wearing a magenta hat with two stupid pom-poms.

Forget it.

I certainly wasn't interested in seeing her. I certainly wouldn't even bother. But before I could turn around and bolt, I felt Mrs. Prattle squeeze my arm.

"Isn't it nice that Ms. Trumpet has taken the time to come see you, Yonder, dear? Isn't that just lovely? Now, why don't we all sit down together in the living room and have a nice chat with your friend?"

Mrs. Prattle caught sight of my expression. "Now, Yonder, dear, let's not be rude, shall we? Mind your manners. Come along, dear; after all, Ms. Trumpet has taken the trouble to travel across town just to see you."

My whole body itched. For a minute I thought that I might just squirm out of my own skin. Who the heck cared if Trudy Trumpet traveled across town, or anywhere else for that matter?

"Yonder?" Mrs. Prattle raised one eyebrow, and I noticed the teacup she was holding rattled on its plate. "Yonder, let's remember that Ms. Trumpet is a very busy woman and that it was very kind of her to take the time to visit you."

When you're a foster child in a foster house, you don't really have any choice in any matters, so sit down we did: Trudy the Terrible, Mrs. Prattle, and Yonder, dear.

It was clear from the start that Trudy had trouble talking. She looked at me, glanced down at her plump hands, looked up again, and began to stutter. I thought I saw her eyes tear.

"Yonder . . ." she began softly. "I'm—I—I'm so . . ."

Trudy looked at me and I looked back at her. My jaw was clenched so hard that my teeth ached. I noticed that Trudy's hands were trembling and that today's hat looked especially ridiculous. All of her hats were stupid, but this was over the top.

"Yonder," Trudy the Terrible finally said, "I'm sorry."

Sorry? So what?

"I didn't realize, I mean I didn't think . . ."

Mrs. Prattle leaned forward. "Are you okay, dear? Can I get you anything? Perhaps a nice cup of ginger tea and a biscuit?"

Trudy shook her head and looked down again. "What I'm trying to say, Yonder, is that I'm sorry that everything happened the way it happened. And I'm really very sorry about your father."

My father? My head whipped around and I looked straight into Trudy the Terrible's green eyes.

What happened to my father? Tell me.

"Yonder," Trudy said softly, "I hate to tell you this, but your father's had a stroke. He was extremely upset to learn that you'd been removed from home and apparently had a terrible, unforeseen reaction, an unfortunate incident. The doctor said his drinking might also be a factor. He's in the hospital downtown."

In the hospital? What was a stroke, anyway? If anything was seriously wrong with my father while I was held against my will in this useless foster home, if anything bad happened to him, then I would—

But before I could do anything, Mrs. Prattle leapt out of her chair to wrap her arms around me. I smelled the evening supper and morning meal on her clothes. For a minute, I felt dizzy and as if I might throw up. Throw up all over Mrs. Prattle's white starched apron or all over Trudy the Terrible's tacky pointed shoes.

Let me go, I wanted to scream, *let me go, let me go, let me go.*

I may have flailed around for a bit then. I may have even swung at Mrs. Prattle and at Trudy too. I don't remember too much of what really happened, but I do remember clearly knowing that I would find my father wherever he was and that I wouldn't waste another single minute of my stupid life in someone else's stupid foster home when I could be by my father's side in our little crooked house with no one to bother us.

Just try to keep me back, I remember thinking as Mrs. Prattle and Trudy called after me and I headed toward the front door. *Just try to keep me back*, I thought as I pushed them away and ran forward. *Just try.*

Thankfully, they didn't.

As Long as It Takes

And so there we were at the hospital again. My father and me. But this time around, this second time, we were staying. How long would my father have to stay?

As long as it takes.

"As long as it takes," reported the first doctor to Mrs. Prattle when she pressed her hands together as if in prayer and asked in the loudest voice imaginable: "So when will he recover? He will recover, won't he? And how long until he's able to return home? After all, we have a child to consider. A precious little child who is terribly upset about all of this."

"How long will he have to be here?" asked Trudy at the hallway nurse's station. "I mean, will he get to go home soon? The kid"—Trudy turned around to take a look at me, double-checking that I was still there—"the poor kid needs her father."

How long? I silently asked the dark green walls in my father's hospital room, where it was hard to breathe. How long until my underwater world returns to the surface again? How long until these doctors fix up my father so he's well? How long until my father looks up, finally fully conscious, and says, "Hey, Yonder. Hey there, darlin', how are you doing, my Yonder girl?"

How long until we sit together again at the kitchen table while he sips his apple cider and I listen to the loud snoring coming from inside the second bedroom where my pony is asleep?

How long until I go home and find Dirt again? How long?

And where is my pony? Where is Dirt? How long does he have until the horsemeat butcher shop truck pulls up in front of Enid's house or animal control finds him wherever the heck he might be? Where he might be hungry, tired, and alone, with no one to take care of him and no one to protect him from harm? How long until my precious pony is sent far away, to distant places unknown? I had to find him. I had to rescue Dirt from who knows what.

Hold on, I counseled Dirt when he seemed frightened or nervous. *It will be okay again soon. Hold on, it won't be long until we can go outside again and you can run free in the meadows and you won't have to hide ever again and the whole entire universe will finally know what a special pony you are and how you were once able to pull me up from down deep so I could finally breathe again.*

When you have a stroke, it means you aren't able to talk for a while. Of course, you may want to talk, to say important things to those you love and to those taking care of you, but you just cannot. Can't. You open your mouth, and nothing comes out. Just air. Air filled with air.

The doctors tried to explain this, but I already understood. Air filled with air. Welcome to my world.

"It's a fairly common medical problem for a man his age," they told Mrs. Prattle, who was squeezing my hands so tightly that I had the urge to shove her away. "And when there's the overlay of the alcohol issue, things tend to get a bit more complicated. In any case, it seems as though he's out of the woods for now."

Mrs. Prattle looked down at me mournfully, her lips moving but without sound. Trudy was wringing her hands.

Of course, the doctors couldn't be absolutely sure why my father had a stroke, although they did say that a sudden shock can be a trigger that makes the human system begin to shut down. But they couldn't explain why he kept drinking and drinking when it made him so ill or why he drank and drank and passed out in his locked bedroom at night, almost every single night since my mother died.

The second doctor, the one with a dark beard and a shaved head, told me that a stroke meant that the blood that flows to the brain gets stuck and stops moving. There is an interruption of blood that limits oxygen and makes brain cells die. When this happens, the bearded doctor said, some parts of the body don't work the same way afterward. When this happens, some things you are used to doing, some things you used to know, get lost.

But my father is already lost, I thought. This was not a thought I usually allowed myself to have, but now it hovered in the air in front of me.

"Don't be scared, Ms. Yonder," the bearded doctor said gently to me later that day after stopping by my father's room. "I think your dad will be fine, but don't be frightened if he seems a little different. Your job will be learning to listen to him in an entirely new way. Do you think you can learn to do that?"

And then he smiled for a moment and looked at me carefully, as if studying my face for clues.

"Are you okay?" he asked quietly. "I know that social services has you under its wing, but it's got to be hard for you not being able to go home with your father until he gets better."

I didn't nod. I didn't shake my head. My face was frozen in a grimace, but the doctor didn't seem to notice.

"Unfortunately," he continued, "your dad might be here for a while, at least until we're sure it's safe for him to leave. And then maybe he will need rehab."

I noticed that there was a little rip at the corner of the doctor's white sleeve.

"Well," he asked kindly, "want to say good-bye to your dad? I'm sure he wants to say good-bye to you."

"Sorry to interrupt, dear." I heard Mrs. Prattle's too-familiar syrupy voice in my ear. "But I brought you a sandwich, Yonder, dear, and a slice of pumpkin pie. Why don't you find a spot in the waiting room to eat, and let me talk to the doctor? These are adult matters, and I don't want you upset."

I shot Prattle a dirty look. Adult matters? Whose father was it, anyway?

I wolfed down the food in the hospital waiting room but didn't taste a bite. I was too sad about my father and too anxious about Dirt. I knew, however, that I couldn't stay in the hospital for a minute longer and I couldn't return to the Prattles' foster house.

I would either drown underwater forever or pop up to the surface and breathe.

Now was the time to take matters into my own hands.

Runaway

Of course, I was aware that Dirt might be long gone despite my plan to save him. I knew he might already be far from home or nestled into someone's sausage casing. But if there was the slightest chance that he was still at large, I'd find him.

Dirt had been there when I needed him most, and I would be there for him now when he needed me. My father was in good hands, and I couldn't help him right now, anyway.

I thought about this, trotting as quickly as possible away from the hospital. It was a clear New England October afternoon, the Vermont days quickly becoming shorter and shorter, and the silhouettes of white clapboard houses were bleary in the setting sun. I shivered, pulling my mother's old jacket tightly against my chest, and couldn't help but wish that I had something warmer to wear. The khaki jacket was soft and comforting, but it never really protected me from the cold.

I made an effort to concentrate on the road ahead, the one that would lead me all the way back to Mutter Street and to the rocky stone path where my empty little crooked house awaited my return.

I had nowhere else to go, runaway or not.

There wasn't anyone I could trust and no one who really trusted me.

Except for Dirt. Except for my pony.

Maybe if I hid out at my house for an hour or so, I could get myself together, gather up some provisions, and think about where to hunt for Dirt. And maybe, just maybe, he was waiting for me there already.

My heart beat faster at the thought.

I realized that someone might have been following me from the hospital, that I wouldn't be completely safe until fully hidden from view. I swallowed hard at the thought of being followed or captured, and I quickly looked over my shoulder to make sure no one was at my back.

To my relief, no one was behind me. Hardly anyone was out on the streets at all this time of evening, children already probably called inside for their dinner, their mothers and fathers awaiting them with open arms.

If I squinted and shaded my eyes with one hand, I could see inside some of the houses' forest-green shuttered front windows, first getting a brief glimpse of a small child seated at a black lacquered piano, then the graceful arches of one room leading to others, reminding me of the ceiling in a castle or church, and finally of two white Sheltie dogs, noses and paws pressed to the glass. It was hard not to wish myself directly into these houses.

It was also hard not to think of my mother. While we never had a castle ceiling or a lacquered piano, when my mother was alive our little crooked house always smelled delicious in the evenings, a pot of potato stew bubbling on the stove or her special tomato soup simmering with bits of cheddar cheese melting on top. And when we had a special night with ice cream from the creamery, she would let me eat it first, before my dinner, so I could enjoy the treat without feeling stuffed. My mother and I would wash the dishes together afterward, sometimes having a soap bubble fight or just standing close, side by side in our warm, steamy family kitchen that was small but that always felt so full.

"It's the self-entitled who feel sorry for themselves when things go badly," Mrs. Prattle had lectured me at the hospital when I refused to look up at her. "The real challenge is to appreciate what you have, dear."

It irritated me when she said that, and it angered me now.

I'd value my own little crooked house if I wanted. I'd always wish for two parents, our own home, and a rocky front lawn where a certain pony could romp and play. If that made me one of the self-entitled, I'd be okay with that.

I didn't want to live at the Prattles' house, no matter how nice they were, or be a part of any pretend family. I just needed my own father back, my own home, and my own pony.

My own island where I could always swim back to shore.

My father, his special cider, his love for me and my mother. All of it.

Dirt, his pesky rascal self. All of that too.

I continued, half walking, half running, dashing quickly past by the Shelter Library, and then by the village bakery, where cheerful Mrs. Snod usually left stale honey bread and corn muffins out back for the birds and stray cats to eat. I may have stopped to collect some of those leftovers myself during those times when my father didn't have work at the orchard. But I didn't have any time now to think about food.

Something rustled from behind a tree. I held my breath and picked up my pace but still could feel the presence of someone coming closer and closer, imagining that the authorities were about to capture me all over again. I broke into a jog, then a run, as I heard the scratching at my heels.

But it was only Walt Whitman, the town stray mongrel, who soon overtook me, his ratty black fur covering both eyes, his black tongue hanging permanently from the left side of a frozen, toothless mouth. As usual, he recoiled when I reached out to pet him.

Soon he softened, allowing me to give him a quick rub on his scabby scalp, and I then quickly wiped my hands on my legs. Walt was known to host all kinds of parasites, and now wasn't the time for me be a warm body for any of them.

I dashed past the town hardware store, the coffee shop, and the Shelter Pharmacy, its rusty sign hanging crookedly from above, the enormous *S* missing so it read HELTER PHARMACY. Dumb. My heart raced as I got closer and closer to home, and I tucked my chin to my chest in the hopes of being less recognizable. At any moment, I could be caught—a terrifying thought.

I kept on going forward as quickly as I could, passing several more houses with white paint chipping and wisteria vines twisted around porch railings, bikes lying on their sides in front yards, lawn grass already yellowing into autumn, huge pots of dark purple mums and bright orange pumpkins lining front steps.

The very same pumpkins that Dirt loved to demolish with abandon.

I broke into a full-out run then, just the thought of Dirt renewing my energy. It wouldn't be long now until I was home.

By the time I get to the wide, hedge-lined blocks of Clearing Avenue, I was running so fast that I almost forgot to make a right turn onto Mutter, through the thicket of evergreens and onto the little rocky path back to my house. But I caught myself just in time to make that hard turn that came up so suddenly.

Almost out of breath, I swiveled around quickly and

again checked to see if I was being followed like some criminal in a mystery book. You never knew, Child and Family Services might just have a department of trench-coated detectives in disguise.

I once read that animals with one eye often end up with improved vision. That losing sight on one side improves the focus of the other. I shivered for a minute, then covered my own left eye with my palm.

The road in front of me shimmered. Soon, I'd be home.

The Little Crooked House

When I finally found myself on the rocky path to the little crooked house, I zoomed all around, calling out in my head for Dirt. I wanted to yell for him with loud, strong words, but they were trapped inside of me with all the other words that I could never say. They rumbled together, pressing against my throat, a furious yearning to shout out for Dirt to return, to come to me, to come home.

But it was hopeless.

I looked behind the evergreens, then inside every thicket, behind each bush. I scoured every inch of land around the house, but there wasn't a single sign of my pony anywhere.

Discouraged didn't cover how I felt.

The sun was just setting, lighting a glimmery trail back

to my front door. Memories tinted the little path like torches. Each and every shaky step on the familiar stones reminded me of steps taken before.

The time I fell and bumped my tooth when I was six and how my mother lifted and held me close.

That tooth is still gray and will be gray forever. "Nothing changes the past," my father told me once. "It is what it is."

The time my father and mother swung me between them, each holding one arm tightly on either side. "Fly," my father had said. "See, Yonder, see how you can fly!" How my mother and father looked at each other then and how they reached across me to kiss from above.

The time I wrestled with Dirt so he wouldn't eat a toad visiting from a nearby pond. Toads are poisonous to ponies. Even a lick will do them in.

But, oddly enough, the little crooked house that finally stood before me at the end of the rocky path was different from the house of my memory from just two days ago. Smaller, frailer—tilted even more to one side than I remembered. In fact, it even looked as though the entire structure might sway and splinter in a strong storm. The house's front plywood stairs were shakier than I remembered too, and as I slowly stepped up toward the front door, I felt them wobble under my feet, suddenly not strong or secure enough to support my weight.

I peered to the left and to the right. No sign of Dirt. I scanned the thicket of trees guarding the house from the road. No movement at all. No evidence of a pony waiting for me to come home.

The loose doorknob jiggled under my touch and the house was unlocked since my father and I never bothered securing it. The door creaked in the exact same way as it always had before Dirt and I were banished to places far and wide.

The first thing I noticed was the odor of must and rotting apple, then the assorted scents of my beloved Dirt: fur, straw, grass, mud, and pony poop.

I swallowed and then swallowed again.

Both bedroom doors were left wide open, something that made me stumble. I was used to closed doors in this little house. I was used to secrets kept behind doors.

When I walked into the second bedroom, I saw that someone had left a shovel, and a pile of hay had been swept into one corner. Maybe my father had done some cleaning before he became ill, but that seemed highly unlikely.

There was the long plastic tub that I used for Dirt's water. There was the bit of hay I used for his food. Only a little bit a day so he wouldn't get fatter.

Not that I ever really managed to avoid this. Glutton was Dirt's middle name.

There was the steel oval grooming brush that I found in the Shelter Goodwill on North Main Street and that I used every single day. "Constant circular strokes are the best," the Muet pony book instructed. "Gentle grooming will keep your pony's coat shining even throughout the winter months."

I had tried to brush Dirt every morning when I got up and every night before bed, and was always surprised how much he seemed to enjoy this activity, settling quietly under my hands. He could be a rebellious pony, but he always loved my touch. I thought of Dirt's thick coat, how it would gather softly under my fingers.

There was the large woolen blue blanket that I took from my father's bed and draped over Dirt's swayed back at night. The tin can of sugar cubes that I fed him, one half cube at a time when he demonstrated his very best beastly behavior. That, of course, was rare.

The windowsill that he gnawed on, the dents in the floor where he stomped, the floorboard that he pulled up one day when I wouldn't let him have any treats—apples, carrots, or sugar. He had been very naughty that day, nipping me on the shoulder, and I was mad.

How I wished to have the chance to be mad at him again. Just one more time. Just to see him again one more time.

I sat down on the floor in Dirt's old room, fingering strands of hay left behind and inhaling the pony fragrance.

My father's bedroom next door was just as it had always been, and I felt my heart heave as I stared at the collection of chipped cups, cans, and bottles strewn across the floor. His one stained pillow rested at the foot of the bed and two gray sheets tumbled together in disarray. A favorite tattered quilt, the one with the burgundy heart-shaped patterns, was rolled into a long mound, a mound inside which a friend, a partner in crime, just might want to hide.

Wishful thinking.

I was tired. My entire body began to buckle, and I found myself stretching out on one side of the bed. Maybe, I thought, maybe if I lay down for a minute, I'd be able to figure things out with a clearer mind. Maybe, if I just closed my eyes for a short second.

Maybe . . .

When I opened my eyes again, my father's room was flooded with light, and I figured that I'd dozed off for the entire night. Not good. Not good at all.

Who knew when the Prattles, Trudy, or the authorities might come looking for me here. It was a miracle that they hadn't showed up already, considering. But they probably figured I'd find a less obvious place to go or were still trying to gather a posse to look for me. In any case, the only thing that mattered now was that I had to find Dirt before either of us was captured again. Speed was going to have to be the name of the game.

But my stomach grumbled. It had been a while since I'd eaten and probably more than eight hours since I'd left the hospital. I peered down to the old wooden floor in the hopes of finding some crackers or half a sandwich. My father rarely ate dinner but often had a snack late at night in bed. No luck.

I had to hurry, and I wasn't looking forward to what I knew I had to do. Since Dirt wasn't anywhere to be found hanging around the little crooked house, my next option was facing old Enid in the flesh. Chances were that Dirt eventually wandered back to her farm after trying to find me at home. And although I hated to admit it, there was even still the possibility that she'd already found him and sold him to a factory. My stomach churned at the thought.

After quickly pocketing two bruised apples from the kitchen counter, four slices of cheese wrapped in cellophane from the refrigerator, and a five-dollar bill and three singles that I kept hidden in the freezer for emergencies, I stopped to look around. There was no telling when I'd see my little crooked house again. Then I headed out the door, running all the way to Enid's farm.

By the time I reached her gate, I had already demolished

one apple and two pieces of cheese, despite my nerves. Running while eating isn't exactly recommended since choking is always a hazard, but I knew that I'd need all the strength and energy I could possibly get.

My stomach began doing somersaults. Who knew what Enid might say or do to me?

I swallowed hard and marched ahead.

Enid Spills the Beans

The old woman was usually seated on her front porch's tarnished glider, gnawing on chewing tobacco and chattering to herself. But didn't it figure—on the one morning that I actually wanted to find her, she was nowhere to be seen.

I knocked on her door. No answer.

I tried to look through her front windows, but they were both covered with old newspapers taped up from the inside.

Just as I was planning to walk around the back of the house, I felt the hair on my neck stand up. Then I heard a low, raspy voice right behind me:

"Why, I'll be! What are you doing here, of all people?"

She was wearing an old pair of stained overalls, a red flannel shirt, and a large straw hat. I felt her bitter breath sting my face as I turned.

"Well, well," she cackled, "Look who it is."

I smiled weakly, trying to dredge up any possible drop of charm I might have, although charm wasn't my strong point.

"The little horse thief herself." Enid's pointy face was wizened, and her beady eyes gleamed. "What do you have to say for yourself, young lady? I'm surprised you had the nerve to show up here. And don't pretend, don't give me that innocent face. I know that you and that drunk of a father had something to do with it when my animal went missing, even before I saw the writing on the wall."

Leave my father out of it. I could feel my cheeks turn the same color as my hair.

"And I have proof too." Enid kicked the porch railing and waved her gnarled hands right in front of my face. "Lucky for you, I didn't go straight to the police. That would have fixed your wagon."

Proof? What kind of proof? I'd been very careful not to let anyone see me sneak Dirt into the house or observe his daily pee outings. Proof wasn't possible.

Enid sneered. Her teeth were brown and looked sharpened, each tooth a tiny knife. "Guess you didn't realize that I knew, did you? Well, I even marched myself down to your shack of a house to have words with your father, but no one was home. Ever heard of telephones? Your father's probably the only person in Shelter without one. Would have saved me a trip."

I wasn't getting anywhere. Minutes were ticking by and still I didn't have any clue of where Dirt had gone. I'd have to step forward now if I wanted to find Dirt. I'd have to make Enid listen to me without saying a single word.

This wasn't going to be easy. It was never easy getting someone to pay attention to silence, but now I simply had to make myself understood. I stood still for a minute, racking my brain for an idea while Enid crossed her arms over her chest and sighed. Her sighs sounded like a train's rumble.

Wait. I suddenly had a brilliant idea that just might work.

I waved my right hand, then pointed to my legs, took another deep breath, and pretended to gallop around the porch like a horse. I pranced faster and faster, feeling like an idiot, determined to make her understand.

"What in the name of God are you doing? Stop that crazy hopping right now or you'll wear the paint right off my front porch!"

The paint was already worn off the porch, so I simply ignored her and continued galloping, pulling at invisible reins. Then I suddenly stopped, mid-gallop, and put my hands on my hips with a questioning expression on my face.

"Oh, I see. I see what you want. You want me to spill the beans about that hellion of a worthless pony, don't you." At least the woman wasn't laughing at me and she understood what I so desperately wanted to know; in fact, her permanent scowl had deepened. I figured that Enid had probably been born with that scowl planted on her face. And then she shot me such an evil look, I stumbled backward as if slapped.

Her eyes lit up a ghoulish greenish color and her mouth tightened into a grimace that made my skin crawl.

For a second, I was tempted to run.

"So, you want to know where that critter is? Why should I tell you? Why should I tell you anything, considering?"

Gathering my composure, I nodded quickly and reached into my pants pocket, where I had stuck my five-dollar bill. When I handed it to Enid, she looked surprised for a minute, and then her face twisted yellow with greediness. She snapped up the money in one second flat and crammed it right inside her flannel shirt. I'm not exactly sure where inside, but I didn't want to think about that.

"I suppose," she continued, crossing her skinny arms, "that I have that lowlife Itty Bitty to thank for finally learning what happened to that worthless horseflesh. Never thought I'd end up dealing with the likes of him! Who would have thought?"

Everyone in Shelter knew about Itty Bitty. Word was that he was from some mysterious island way up north by Canada, where everyone was a cannibal, gobbling each other up every chance they got, and that he'd been in jail for knifing a man up Tattler Falls when he was a teenager. Heywood Prune once told me that Itty swallowed whole animals raw, heads, hooves, and claws included. I didn't actually believe that, considering the source, but the very idea made me shudder. And it made me sick to think that this criminal had anything to do with Dirt.

"So, little missy." Enid seemed to be enjoying herself now, smacking her wrinkled lips and chortling. I thought her chortles sounded just like croaking frogs. "Why, just late yesterday evening, that Itty Bitty varmint came up to the farm for a visit, and offered me cold, hard cash for the animal right then and there. Said something about keeping the critter and maybe giving it to some kind of circus or zoo. Pretty foolish, if you ask me, since that animal's uglier than sin. Anyway, since the horse was missing and no one had seen him, I couldn't sell, now, could I? Could I?"

A zoo or circus? It was a huge relief that Dirt was still alive and I didn't have to worry about horsemeat anymore. But the idea of him dressed up in silly costumes and used for entertainment bothered me. While Dirt wasn't exactly dignified, he wouldn't like doing circus tricks or being pointed at by crowds.

It seemed that Enid was waiting for me to answer her question. No chance of that.

"But you know what, you little thief?" Enid bent down toward me then, her voice rising a few pitches. "Itty Bitty knew just where to find my horse. He'd seen a redheaded girl walking it in the overgrowth across the way a few days ago, just like some fool walking a darn dog. He saw you there with my horse behind your house a while ago too. 'A redheaded girl leading a short, fat horse'—those were his exact words."

Shetland pony, not horse. My eyes narrowed so that they were almost closed and I bit my lips, once then twice.

"And do you know what else, you pathetic juvenile delinquent?" the old biddy continued, spitting out each word. "We made a deal right then and there, Itty Bitty and me. Got myself some cash and that fool Bitty fella, well, he bought that dumb creature from me, thank goodness for that, half a bag of feed included. Itty went and found him right behind your house, clear as day."

Dirt wasn't a dumb animal, and he certainly wasn't uglier than sin. He was a Shetland pony from Scotland. And it broke my heart to learn that Dirt might have been waiting for me at home. Innocently waiting, with no idea of what was to come.

"Now, get out of here, you wretched pain in the neck. You and your father are one and the same. Both of you losers, no good at all."

Enid slammed the door right in my face, and I heard the sound of it bolting shut.

I may have been a horse thief, but I resented being called a loser. My father and I walked a different road than most, but we knew better than to slam a door right in someone's face.

Tiny Mysteries

I knew how to pick locks.

One of my father's friends from the orchard had taught me last year. All it took was an extra-large safety pin and some know-how. If Itty Bitty had locked my pony in some barn or padlocked him to a post outside, it wouldn't be a problem to free him. No problem at all. As I rushed down the road away from Enid's farm, I thought about all the possibilities. I was getting closer. It wouldn't be long now until I found my pony, my own Dirt. Unless he was already performing in some circus tent or was behind bars at a zoo. But there wasn't any time to worry about that.

Everyone in town knew that Itty Bitty lived at the very end of Bellow, at the far corner of Mutter, in a white trailer right by the Shelter town dump, and all the children were to stay as far away as possible. A long time ago, when I was small, my father and I would see Itty picking through the trash while we searched for old car parts, an enormous, lonely figure walking through garbage. For years, my father collected thrown-away parts at the dump in the hopes of one day putting together a car or truck for my mother. This never happened.

Shelter kids were frightened by Itty Bitty, and for good reason. He was a gigantic man, about twenty or thirty years old, but his actual age was hard to tell because of his massive size—he was enormously tall and enormously strong. At Robert Frost Middle School, Heywood Prune was fond of calling Itty "King Kong" and scaring the kids in class by telling all kinds of Itty Bitty monster stories. Of course, I wasn't spooked in the least by any of Prune's stupid tales but was more than concerned about the thought of the huge man being mean to Dirt. Let's just say that he wasn't the kind you'd ever want to meet face-to-face. Even so, I raced down Bellow Avenue at a breakneck pace. The sooner I rescued Dirt, the better. I wanted to make sure that he didn't turn into one of Itty Bitty's afternoon meals.

When I finally reached the town dump, I slid to a stop. It was a gray, chilly day and the dump was covered in an eerie light, kind of a hazy green-purple, the color of a bruise not quite ready to heal. I could see the white trailer glinting in between dark mounds of trash and thought how odd it was that such a huge man lived in such a tiny house. A gust of wind suddenly blew over me, and the odor of garbage smacked me right in the face.

When I was a little kid, I thought it exciting to root around the dump with my father and didn't realize it was such a sad place, full of old things thrown out and forgotten. Now I saw that the dump was a place where things ended, not where they began.

It's now or never, I thought, mobilizing my strength of mind and body. *Now is the time to face Itty Bitty in person.* And just at that very moment, as if on cue, it began to rain and then thunder. That's when I squared my shoulders and marched directly ahead, right through the center of the Shelter town dump.

By the time I reached the little trailer, I was drenched. The thunder had stopped, but cold rain continued to fall without a break. I surveyed the house in front of me and then tried to see what was in back. If Itty had bought Dirt from Enid as she insisted, where was he keeping my pony? It certainly wasn't in this tiny trailer, for heaven's sake, and there wasn't any evidence of a pony outside.

Dredging up every ounce of nerve, I reached up to the trailer's black door and hesitated. The rain blurred my vision, reminding me of the very first day Dirt came to my own little house and how I'd hardly been able to make out his shape. My hand was slippery with rain, but I squeezed it into a fist and knocked. Once, then twice.

No answer. I knocked again.

And just as I was ready to give up waiting for Itty to answer his door, I heard a woman's high voice from inside.

"Can I help you?" the woman asked.

I spun around to answer, and to my shock and surprise, there wasn't a woman standing in front of me at all, but Itty Bitty himself in the flesh.

The man was enormous. He was wearing a brightly colored, short-sleeved Hawaiian shirt and low-slung plaid pants; actually, on closer look, they appeared to be plaid pajama bottoms with unraveling hems. A dark-blue bandana held his stringy hair off his forehead, and the rest trailed down all the way to his shoulders.

I reluctantly followed Itty Bitty as he shuffled ahead, and pressed my fingernails into my hands until they hurt. My parents had both warned me against going into a stranger's house, and I was aware that I was probably making a terrible mistake. My stomach galloped in such fast circles that I had to steady myself against a wall before moving forward. But it was raining too hard to get any answers on the trailer's front steps, and when Itty asked me inside, I really didn't have a choice. Not if I didn't want to drown. Not if I wanted to find Dirt.

The surprising thing was that Itty Bitty's voice was high-pitched like a child's and musical as a girl's. If I wasn't so terrified, I might have found this funny, that such a huge man sounded so small. His speech definitely didn't match his size, and I had to bend forward in order to understand his soft words.

"Sit down, little girl." I looked around the trailer quickly, shivering from the cold rain. Itty Bitty's home was just as I might have imagined, the narrow slits of windows covered with brown wrapping paper, and a thick layer of grime everywhere. I sat down on an old beanbag chair that was torn at the center, spilling its innards all over the soiled floor, and watched closely as Itty slowly lowered himself onto a lopsided, dark-blue vinyl couch. He had to grab on to the couch's armrest in order to make it all the way down, then carefully, painfully, wobbled himself into place. There was a loud hiss as he settled, a cloud of dust escaping under his weight.

I looked at Itty Bitty's wide face and saw that the left cheek was etched with a pitch-black tattoo. Seeing me stare, he reached up to gently touch the curved drawing that wound up to his eye and nodded.

"Kanaloa," he said quietly. "God of the sea, protector of sea travelers. Got it a long time ago, after getting locked up for things I shouldn't have done. Want something to eat, little girl?"

Itty Bitty's features were large and flat, watery blue eyes covered by folds of skin and low, thick eyebrows; a wide nose that almost looked smashed on one side; full, ash-gray lips; and perfectly round flushed cheeks. His long hair was inky, and his pockmarked skin was blotched gray and bloated around the chin and neck, as if it had been soaked underwater. The skin of a dolphin or seal.

He looked like someone who lived beneath.

I shook my head in response to his offer of something to eat, but he still reached behind the couch to a narrow table where there were three yellow boxes of what looked to be lemon-drop cookies, and without even shifting in place, he poured a pile of cookies into his gigantic hand.

Lemon-drop cookies happen to be my favorite, but I was too nervous to consider taking a bite.

Itty's trailer was crammed with mounds and mounds of books and old magazines. It took me a minute to notice this, as I thought at first that the mounds were trash. On second look, however, it was clear that this strange man collected volumes of all kinds: hardback, paperback, even large, fancy books with once-shiny covers, now torn at the corners. As my eyes cleared from the dust, I saw that almost every inch of the trailer's floor was covered by a book or magazine of some kind.

Strange for a hardened criminal. But I figured that when it comes to it, most people are the same. They want to know things. They want to understand all the mysteries of the world. That's why I loved libraries and books, after all.

I leaned forward in my beanbag chair and he leaned back into the couch, both of his arms spread wide, as if supporting himself.

"You came to ask me something, little girl?"

I nodded.

The massive man was quiet for a minute, and I couldn't help but think about the fastest route out the front door. Maybe Itty was thinking about how to tie me up for slaughter or where he might keep me as a permanent prisoner. I felt the hair on my arms and on the back of my neck prickle. My whole body hummed with fear.

"So you're the girl without words," Itty finally said after a few long minutes, looking at me carefully, as if to assess my size and if I might be a tasty tidbit for his dinner. "I know about you."

My eyes might have bugged out and my lower lip quivered. What did Itty Bitty know about me and how did he know it? I wasn't exactly a public figure in Shelter.

"Must be pretty hard," the enormous man continued. "Must be pretty hard to get what you want when you can't even ask for it." Then he stuffed his pile of cookies into his mouth with one quick motion. When he chomped down, bits of yellow icing flew in the air. "Yup, must be hard to get what you want."

For a minute, I thought I might cry. My eyes filled up for a second and I felt a stinging in my throat. It *was* hard to ask and to let others know what I wanted. But I had no choice anymore. I had to step up and be heard, even though I didn't talk.

We looked at each other then, Itty Bitty and me. We

both took deep breaths at the same time and stared at each other until I just couldn't look anymore. When I absolutely couldn't stand it another single second, I stood up, and with my index finger, I slowly, carefully wrote out a huge word in the dusty air. I made sure that each air letter was clear enough to understand.

P-O-N-Y

Itty looked confused.

I wrote out the word again, this time larger.

P-O-N-Y

"Ynop?" Itty still looked bewildered but tried to pronounce the word I had written, his mouth full of cookies. "Ynop?"

Couldn't the man read a simple word, for heaven's sake?

But then I quickly realized that I had written the letters backward, from *my* left to right, instead of from his. I turned around, extended my hand so Itty could see, and wrote the word in the air all over again.

"Ah." Itty laughed in a high, girlish chuckle. "That pony. You want to know what happened to the pony. I knew you were going to ask me about that."

I spun around and nodded vigorously, then sat down again, waiting eagerly to hear his response.

"Yup, I figured that's what you want to find out, about that funny-looking critter. I figured that out the minute I saw you at my door. And, you know, the farm lady told me how someone stole that critter. Boy, she was mad. I heard that she was selling it for some bucks and so walked up there to her farm myself." He sighed deeply, as if remembering the journey.

I was getting frustrated. It seemed as if getting information from Itty might take the entire afternoon. I'd never known anyone to speak so slowly.

Itty Bitty chuckled and wiped his mouth with his sleeve. "You know," he said, drawing out each word with his musical, lilting voice, "you may be just a young girl, but I see you got nerve. I know you stole that pony and you kept it before it got away. I know it wasn't yours to keep or sell."

I was terrified then. I could see the dark bubbling up in Itty's light-blue eyes. He knew all about me. He knew all about my sins.

Itty and I exchanged glances, but his face was expressionless. I couldn't tell if he was about to yell at me for my crime or swallow me whole.

And where was Dirt? I still hadn't found out anything of help.

"So," Itty continued, "after that farm lady put up the meat sign, I figured it was my time to count my dollars. I knew I could make some cash by selling that animal myself, right under her nose."

Under her nose? What was he talking about?

I was leaning forward then, Itty still leaning back on the couch. If he made a sudden move, something very unlikely considering his heft, I could beat it right out the door. But I sure wasn't leaving unless I had to, at least until I found out exactly what he had done with Dirt.

"You know," he continued, looking down at his meaty knees, "I have a brother, Carlo, living way up one town north. He's a pretty slick character, my brother, and opened a petting zoo this year, right up there next to his cabin on the corner of South Stammer Road in Holler Hollow."

A petting zoo? My heart dropped and flooded at the same time. Is that what Enid meant?

"He was looking to buy new animals all of a sudden," Itty continued. "Seemed like he wanted a bunch of new ones for his zoo. But that turned out to be a lie." Itty looked crestfallen, and I was confused. "Didn't know about that lie at first."

But what did this have to do with Dirt?

"So, I gave the old lady twenty bucks for the pony to sell it the next day to Carlo for thirty. Thought I'd make myself ten dollars in a wink of an eye."

Itty winked at me as if to demonstrate.

I didn't see the humor in the situation, although the idea of a petting zoo was certainly much better than a circus. Maybe Dirt was happily nibbling on caramel popcorn while crowds of children lined up to pet his velvet nose. Maybe his blond mane was braided up in pretty ribbons and there were other ponies to play with. Maybe. And if that was the case, I certainly hoped that someone was paying attention to his diet so he wouldn't overeat. Too much caramel popcorn couldn't be good for a pony.

"That pony is up by Holler Hollow with my brother, Carlo," Itty said. "At least I think he's still there. But if you want to see him, you'd better get moving right quick. Still some time."

Time? Time for what?

"Carlo said the zoo's closed down now so I'm not sure what he's going to do with his animals—your pony too."

I'd been to Holler Hollow a few times with my father since he worked at the orchard just south of the little town. But how could I find Dirt in time since he'd been taken so far away, and how could I get there before the zoo moved on? Holler Hollow was about a half an hour drive, if I remembered right.

At least I knew where I might find Dirt and that he wasn't being digested in someone's stomach with a side of home fries. My heart expanded for a moment, as if blown up wide, then shrank down again, leaking air. The thought of Dirt disappearing again hit my chest like a ton of bricks.

"And do you know what?" Itty shook his head and looked at me imploringly, as if he thought I might just answer. "My own brother, Carlo, my own flesh and blood, just loaded up that pony into his trailer without paying me a penny after all my trouble. He told me that the town closed down his zoo, and he didn't have any money but that he'd take the pony off my hands. I told him no, no way. But my brother just laughed. Without another word. My own brother stole that pony from me without another word and without giving me the cash. And when you can't trust your own brother, well, nothing much makes sense."

For a second, Itty's entire face collapsed. He shook his head and looked down at his hands.

But I really couldn't blame him for buying and trying to sell Dirt. He hadn't done anything wrong. I was the one responsible for putting Dirt in danger. I was the one who the authorities were looking for, and I was the one who caused my pony to run away.

I saw how hurt Itty Bitty was that his own brother let him down. I could see that he was sad. And so I reached out my hand all the way over to where the big man was sitting. I wanted to let him know that I forgave him and to thank him for telling me the truth. At least finally, I knew where my beloved pony had gone.

Itty looked confused for a minute, as if nobody had offered to shake his hand in a very long time. But instead of offering his own hand in response, he slowly, very slowly, stood up.

"You're a special girl. I see that." Itty towered over me, but I wasn't scared of him anymore. "There aren't many Shelter folk who come see me here in my home, or care about any animal."

I was standing too, facing this giant of a man. Well, not really facing, since he was practically double my height. I arched my neck, looked up into his dark, tattooed face, and noticed that Itty Bitty's eyes had softened, and when he gazed down at me, they crinkled at the corners. I blinked. It was as if his eyes were splashed with sadness, and so I understood that Itty Bitty was lonely and might need a friend.

Without stopping to think, I wrapped my arms around Itty's huge, billowing stomach and gave him a swift hug. My arms didn't quite make it all the way around, but he patted me on the back quickly, and then on top of my head.

"You know, little girl"—Itty stepped back to look down at me again—"I have a book to show you." And then from a tall pile in front of the couch, he pulled out a thick volume with a ripped but still glossy cover. It was a beautiful rose-colored book, thick and heavy, and I knew without looking any further that it would have delicate, crinkling tissue paper separating the illustrations inside, and covered watercolor illustrations. I had never read this particular one, although I always meant to: *Black Beauty* by Anna Sewell.

"This is a story about a horse," he said, "and I won't tell you the end. But there's all kinds of adventures and tiny mysteries inside." Itty looked right into my face, and I held my breath. "Friends and travelers help that horse like I wish I could help you. I'm sorry that I can't bring you back your pony, little girl."

Itty Bitty handed me the book, treating it as carefully as something alive. I could almost see the pages quiver, kind of like a fluttery breath, but knew that simply couldn't be.

I stared at the enormous man, and he stared right back at me. I saw Itty Bitty's entire heart rise up in his chest, slipping all the way out into the dusty room. It hung for a minute like a balloon in the thick air. Itty Bitty's heart was huge, and I wished that I could tie it on a string to my wrist so it could trail behind me, way up high.

I touched *Black Beauty* with my fingertips as if to read it in Braille, then returned it to Itty's enormous hands. I would read this book one day soon, and when I did, I would remember how Itty Bitty and I became friends.

The Gray Shed

I really didn't want to go back to the little crooked house that night since the authorities might be looking for me there by now. But it would be getting late before long, and I needed to find somewhere to stay for the night. Although facing Enid again was the last thing I wanted to do, I remembered that there was an old shed at the far end of her property, somewhere she rarely went, day or night. So I hightailed it right back to where I came from, a short but still tiring walk.

When I snuck under Enid's wire fence and pulled open the shed door, I realized that I hadn't thought about how cold it might get during the night. Standing still for a minute, I inhaled dust and something else hard to identify. Maybe oil, the kind you use to pour into a truck or use to loosen rusted hinges. The shed seemed pretty solid, with a concrete floor and some sort of paneling for walls.

There was even a lightbulb hanging from the ceiling, but I knew better than to turn it on, in case Enid might be alerted. I took a slow step forward, and felt a cobweb slip across my face. No problem there; I was used to spiders and their webs.

Something skittered across my feet. I gulped. I didn't mind mice outside in the fields, but something about them being inside gave me the willies. The floor creaked as I stepped forward. And then my eyes adjusted to the dark.

The shed was filled with tools and shovels of every kind imaginable, a snowblower and a green-and-yellow John Deere ride-on mower. I was surprised to see the lawn mower, as I knew the old woman had goats to keep the grass trimmed, unless she ended up selling them for sausage as well. Was there such a thing as goat sausage? I shivered at the thought.

Luckily for me, someone had left an old navy parka hanging from a nail behind the shed door, but when I picked it up, it felt stiff to the touch as if left out in the rain. No problem; I shook out the jacket with both hands, feeling the crusty fabric soften under my touch, then immediately searched both pockets for hidden treasures. Eureka! Wouldn't you know, there was a ten-dollar bill in the left pocket, more money than I had ever had in my possession at one time! And it wasn't really stealing, was it, I thought as I stuffed the bill into my own pants pocket and threw out the crushed cigarette found along with the money. The ten-dollar bill had been forgotten, hadn't it, and I most definitely needed the cash more than the person who carelessly left it behind. I'd have to buy something to eat before too long.

The parka was so large that I almost could wrap it around myself twice, but not quite. It was lined with red flannel and even had a hood, so I figured I would be warm enough through the cold fall night. But as I sat down, cross-legged, on the hard, cold floor, I still felt a sudden rush of pure terror. Here I was, all alone in the dark, my clothes still damp from the rain, and without a clear plan of what to do next.

What if I couldn't find Dirt in Holler Hollow, and how would I even get there in the first place? The town was a full half an hour away by car, and that would take me forever to walk. I wrapped the parka around myself as tightly as I could manage and laid my head on a large burlap sack of feed stored in a corner. It didn't really matter how long it would take to get to Holler Hollow. No matter what, I would find my way there.

Remembering that there was one apple and one piece of cheese left crammed in my pants pocket, I inhaled them quickly, then was thirsty for something—anything— to drink. I'd seen a rusty faucet on an outside corner of the shed but figured I should wait until later before going outside again. And I'd have to pee soon, anyway, so I would get a drink and relieve myself in the bushes at the same time, after it was fully dark. The last thing I needed was Enid finding me watering her property au naturel.

I shifted my legs to one side, then snuggled up against

the burlap pillow of feed. As I closed my eyes, I thought of the oncoming Shelter winter, one of my favorite times of year, although most everyone in town dreaded it. Here I was, all alone in the damp, my clothes wet, the shed getting colder by the minute, and I still yearned for the frosted sparkle of a clear winter day. I even loved the freezing nights; when, snuggled in a blanket, you could hear the crush of wild animals as they stumbled in icy snow. Their hooves crackled through the frozen surface, then plunged into a hushed belly of white. That's where calm lived for me, not in spoken language but under, below, in the deep.

I know it sounds crazy, but only Dirt meets me there in that silent place: our battered hearts buried but still thumping.

When I woke up the next morning, it was barely light outside, and for a moment I thought I heard a pony's soft bray. But it was only the sound of Enid's enormous hog, Arthur, who was soon to be carved up into the old woman's winter hams. She had told me so herself at the Shelter fair last summer when Arthur won the prize for the largest hog in the county.

I listened to old Arthur snorting around outside the shed and felt sad for a moment. He wasn't a mean hog, after all, and it seemed unfair that his life wouldn't add up to more than a few meals on mean Enid's dinner table. Well, maybe more than a few.

My forehead was throbbing, it felt like someone was hammering it from the inside out. And my neck wasn't feeling so good either, having been cramped all night on a cold sack of feed. I stood up gingerly, slowly moving my head side to side, stretching out my arms and legs, but quickly sitting down again. It was then that I remembered I had barely eaten anything the night before and that my body might be in official starvation mode. Quickly, I pulled out the last piece of cheese from my pants pockets and took a small bite. Ms. Muet's book on ponies clearly specified that it's important for them to be fed slowly when in starvation mode so they don't end up with belly bloat, and I figured that might apply to me as well. I took tiny bites. I chewed carefully. The cheese seemed to soothe my head, nevertheless, as well as my grumbling stomach, and before I knew what was what, all of it was gone. So much for Ms. Muet's advice.

Impatient to get going, I was tempted to start on my way but decided it might be safer to delay until I was ready to leave the shed for good, since I wanted to limit the chances of being seen. First, I needed to get my wits together and decide how in the heck I would get myself all the way to Holler Hollow.

The John Deere mower caught my eye. I had been raised on tractors and lawn mowers during the years my father worked on this very farm for a living. He hadn't always just picked apples at the orchard, but also used to moonlight, helping Enid keep her property in shape. That was before she fired him for drinking on the job.

Being an expert on such things, I knew that driving a tractor or lawn mower on a public road was illegal. It would take forever, anyway, to make my way to Holler Hollow in such an unconventional manner; not exactly a practical choice. For a minute, I had to grin, imagining myself chugging along Vermont Route 9, all the way to Holler Hollow, at one mile per hour. It would be faster if I walked.

A bicycle would have been perfect, or even cross-country skis if I had them and there was snow on the ground. Unfortunately, that wasn't the case, and neither was available, anyway. There was only one answer to my predicament: I would have to try to find a ride.

I knew that this was a stupid idea because anyone offering me a ride would probably be someone who knew me, and that presented a problem, to say the least. Anybody who recognized me most definitely would want to know why I wasn't in school and why I was heading north all by myself. But just maybe an apple picker from the orchard, someone who worked with my father, wouldn't ask too many questions; it wasn't as if I could answer them, anyway.

It was just getting light outside and the day was just about to begin. I would have to take my chances.

The Daring Trip
to Holler Hollow

I had borrowed the navy parka I found in Enid's gray shed
and pulled up the hood over my head for disguise. After all,
I was a wanted woman. A wanted girl, to be precise. And I
must have looked a mite peculiar, a short figure in an over-
size jacket, enormous hood covering my forehead and cheeks.
Only my eyes and nose protruded, my mouth also hidden
since the parka was zipped up as far as it could possibly go.

I had decided to plant myself in front of Ernie's Gas and
Go, since Ernie had two pumps and it was the last gas station before the interstate. I plopped down on the dark-green
peeling bench just outside the little store and waited for I
didn't really know what. It wasn't as if a van was going to
drop down from the sky and whiz me northward.

A few folks came and went, most not even noticing a bundle of a girl sitting nervously on the wooden bench.

Tommy Belcher from the fire station stopped to give me a quick "Hi there, kiddo," but he was on foot, probably just getting a pack of cigarettes from Ernie's. It seemed strange to me that a fireman would smoke.

A few dumb teenage boys flew in and out of the store, laughing like idiots and clutching what probably was an illegal six-pack of beer, even though it was still morning. Probably skipping school, just like me. Ernie's daughter was known to sell to underage kids when she was working at the cash register during her morning shift.

A few truckers stopped to gas up, then a man with a flat tire. I watched him change his tire as if he'd never done it before. He huffed and puffed, taking what must have been close to thirty minutes just to get on the road again. My father could have done it in five.

It was starting to get late, no telling how long I'd been sitting there on that dumb bench, but the morning sun was already rising toward noon. Just as I was about to give up and figure out another plan to get to Holler Hollow, a huge white SUV swung into Ernie's.

The woman inside leaned out her window. Her hair was perfectly coiffed, shellacked into a blond bob, gold earrings sparkling, and her mouth outlined in bright red. She was wearing a navy blazer.

"Hi there, lovey," she called to me. "Do you know where I could find a coffee shop? I'm not from around here."

No kidding.

I nodded, then pointed to Ernie's store. There was usually a pot or two of coffee brewing on one of the rusted hot plates.

The woman motioned for me to come closer with an elegant wave, her fingernails painted bright red. A diamond bracelet lit up her left wrist, which was smothered in a bundle of gold bangles.

"Sweetheart," she said in what sounded like a Southern drawl, "sweetheart, would you mind going inside and buying me a cup of coffee? I so desperately need one but I can't leave my kitty alone in the car. Here's a couple of dollars for the trouble and another two for the coffee."

It was only then I noticed that a white cat was curled on the woman's lap. She caught me looking and smiled.

"This is little Cuddles Ross," she said, fluffing up the cat's fur. "Isn't she pretty? And my name's Ms. Marilyn Ross. I really do appreciate your help with the coffee."

I really didn't think that Ernie or his daughter would care a hoot about a cat in the store.

Cuddles began to meow, once then twice.

"Oh no, not again!" Ms. Ross looked annoyed. "Cuddles has had to do her poo-poo business already three times on this trip and we've only been on the road for a few hours.

I think that the poor dear's carsick. And now I'm late for my meeting. Oh my."

I hadn't realized that cats were allowed at business meetings.

"Sweetie, do you happen to know how far it is to Blatherham? I'm trying to make it before one. Here, don't forget your money."

And just as I reached for the welcome cash, Cuddles hissed loudly and I jumped back despite myself, quickly withdrawing my hand. Angry cats shouldn't be messed with.

Then Cuddles crouched down on her haunches, shot me an evil glance, and whoosh, she flew off her owner's lap all the way through the open window.

"Good gracious, oh no, Cuddles, come right back! Oh dear, my goodness, stop, stop, stop!"

By then the white puff of fur was already headed straight behind Ernie's into the fields, Ms. Ross dashing after her toward the corn rows, business suit and all.

I could have done the right thing. I could have helped catch the mischievous little rascal. After all, I was a lover of animals, no matter how small, and Ms. Ross had just offered to give me some much-needed cash. But my rescue mission was a priority. I had to find Dirt. So without giving the matter any more thought, I scooted right into the SUV's backseat. Thank goodness the car was large, with plenty of extra room, and I climbed all the way into the hatchback, quickly laying myself flat.

Holler Hollow was on the way to Blatherham. Here was my chance; finally a safe transport.

Getting out of the SUV at Holler Hollow was another matter, but I'd worry about that later. That was, if the woman and her runaway pet ever returned.

It seemed forever until Ms. Ross and Cuddles finally came back; I was beginning to worry that they had gotten lost—the cornfields can be confusing if you're chasing a cat.

"You're a very bad kitty cat." I heard Ms. Ross's voice again as the car door opened, the scent of her flowery perfume filling the car. "Now, sit here like a good girl, and I don't want to hear another peep."

The cat spat out a hiss in objection. I didn't blame her. It wasn't the cat's fault if her belly was upset.

Ms. Ross quickly pulled onto the highway without checking where I'd gone, kind of like I'd never existed at all. I wondered whether she'd even give me a second thought.

Lying on the hatchback on the hard car floor, I couldn't believe how bold I'd been to stow away in a stranger's car. My armpits were damp and my hands slick with sweat. To tell the absolute truth, I was perspiring buckets as we sped along. What had I done; how the heck would I make it out of the SUV in the nick of time?

I knew that the trip to Holler Hollow should take thirty minutes or so, but it would be difficult to tell time without a clock or watch. There was something I read once about tracking the sun and that using a shadow stick could mark the passage of hours. Since neither was very practical for someone in my plight, I just started counting seconds, then minutes, to gauge my whereabouts. That didn't last long, however, since I kept losing my place and having to start all over again.

A black leather briefcase trembled in the hatchback, a flashlight and a silver thermos rolled about, but nothing useful caught my eye. Nothing that would help me make an escape when the time came.

Suddenly, I remembered that there was a Dairy Queen on the right side of the road, just before getting to Holler Hollow and not far from the orchard where my father worked. If I kept my eyes open for the Dairy Queen, I figured I would know that it was time to make it quickly out of the car.

So, for the first time in a few days, I felt myself relax. I had thirty minutes to lie back in Ms. Ross's fancy car and watch the world zoom on by. The leaves on passing trees had already begun to fall and I could see stretches of bright red and yellow swirling outside the window like confetti. The car was warm and toasty, and I was just where I was supposed to be, on my way to rescue Dirt.

I lay there on the car floor, contemplating my good fortune and quick decision-making skills. If I hadn't acted quickly and jumped into the back of the SUV, who knew where I'd be or when I'd find my pony. I felt pretty proud of myself then, pleased to have finally acted on what I knew to be right.

Suddenly, I heard Cuddles scratching loudly from the front seat and Ms. Ross's scolding words:

"Now, stop that, you bad girl," my driver was muttering. "You're ruining the leather. Don't make me sorry that I brought you along. You promised to be a good girl, remember? Remember?"

But Cuddles didn't seem to have any memory of that particular conversation, and started to scratch even harder than before. Then she suddenly leapt from the front to perch on the backseat's headrest. She looked down at me coolly as I lay hidden on the trunk floor below, Ms. Ross calling out plaintively for the cat to return to her side. But Cuddles was stubborn, ignoring each plea, clearly more interested in staring at me.

"Well, okay, Cuddles, if that's how you want to be. But don't come meowing to me when you want a scratch behind the ears. I can't pet you if you insist on staying in the back of the car."

Cuddles didn't budge. I wondered if Ms. Ross always talked to her cat in that babyish way. But finally, there was some quiet.

All of a sudden, the car veered to the left quickly, perhaps to change lanes, and Cuddles landed smack on my face.

My position was uncomfortable, to say the very least. It's not easy to lie still with a furry rear blocking your air. Somehow Cuddles had ended up in that unfortunate pose, her tail and her you-know-what covering my nose and mouth. Her claws dug into my neck and chest, making me grit my teeth in pain. But I could tell by Cuddles's frozen stance that she was frightened and that she didn't quite know what to do. So I reached up with one hand to stroke her with a gentle touch, and Cuddles, the wicked puffball, started to purr. She swiveled around quickly so we were face-to-face.

We rode together like that for a while, just Cuddles and me, my hand on her back, her fur warm against my skin.

Had I fallen asleep? I opened my eyes with alarm. What if we'd passed Holler Hollow and I'd have to find another ride going the opposite direction? I sat up for a minute and looked out the window for the Dairy Queen or anything that would indicate where we were. Cuddles hissed, clearly annoyed that I'd forgotten her.

Ms. Ross suddenly braked at a light. While I didn't see the Dairy Queen, I knew we must be close to the Holler Hollow outskirts, since the highway didn't have any other stops. Cuddles licked my chin with her rough tongue and I bolted upright, pressing down on the trunk's release button as quickly as I could. It popped open immediately, so I saluted my furry friend, then slid out the back of the SUV, closing the back door as softly as possible.

Thank goodness there weren't any cars behind us or my goose might have been cooked. As it was, I ran to the curb without Ms. Marilyn Ross knowing I had left or that she had aided and abetted a juvenile delinquent who was on the run.

At least, that's what I thought. As it turned out, I heard Ms. Ross's high voice calling out to me as I dashed ahead. But I wasn't going to stop for anyone or anything. I was on my way to find Dirt.

Holler Hollow

Holler Hollow was even smaller than Shelter and so I knew it wouldn't be too hard to find Itty Bitty's brother's zoo on South Stammer Road. I walked briskly down the hill toward town, past the WELCOME TO HISTORIC HOLLER HOLLOW, POP. 2000 sign, three old brick mill buildings that looked abandoned, the glass in their windows smashed, a Wendy's drive-through, and then stopped at a mini-mart that caught my eye. One of those places with a giant cardboard cutout of a Big Cherry Fizz taped to the window.

Cherry Fizzes are disgusting. They taste like cough syrup.

Fingering the ten-dollar bill in my pocket, I decided to buy a packet of Nabisco cheese-sandwich crackers and a can of Coke. But first I had to find a bathroom. The clerk seemed to eye me suspiciously as I dashed to the back of the store where the bathroom was fortunately unlocked. I did my business as quickly as possible. The bathroom was very small, and it smelled exactly like the one at Robert Frost Middle School. Not a pleasant memory.

Next I bought my two items at the mini-mart's front counter, and figured that I must have been quite a sight. A girl with bright-red hair, wearing a man's blue parka and covered with road dust from head to toe. I didn't care. All I knew was that I needed a bit of nourishment before heading out to find the petting zoo and rescue Dirt.

As I left the mini-mart, I noticed a few other shops lined up side by side, one with an enormous plastic bottle of maple syrup tilted above its baby-blue door (not difficult to figure out what was being sold there), another with a sign that read PAWS AND CLAWS, J. HERRIOT, DVM (whatever the heck *DVM* meant), and a third that was a hardware store of some sort. Wheelbarrows, shovels, straw brooms, and an arrangement of black ice scrapers sat out on its front porch, a bulletin board of community notices hanging from a post hook. I stopped for a moment to look at the various notices and flyers.

The bulletin board notices were typical, the same as I'd seen many times at Village Market back home in Shelter: BABY-SITTER WANTED, BABYSITTER AVAILABLE, ADORABLE BLACK KITTENS FOR SALE, MRS. ROMANOVICH'S EXOTIC PETTING ZOO, STOREFRONT FOR RENT ON MAIN, LOST COLLIE . . .

Wait.

I blinked and took a deep breath, then scanned the bulletin board notice again: Mrs. Romanovich's Exotic Petting

Zoo? Had I read that correctly? Could it be that the small town of Holler Hollow had more than one petting zoo? Doubtful. I looked carefully at the flyer advertising the exotic zoo, then quickly pulled it down from two rusted thumbtacks. It was torn and frayed, printed on orange paper, and the picure of the tiger made me gulp.

MRS. ROMANOVICH'S EXOTIC PETTING ZOO

41 S. STAMMER ROAD

COME SEE ANIMALS FROM ALL OVER THE WORLD!

$3 FOR ADULTS $1 CHILDREN UNDER 10

NO DOGS ALLOWED   NO PUBLIC RESTROOMS

There was no doubt about it. The one and the same. Hadn't Itty Bitty described his brother's zoo on South Stammer Road? But who in the world was Mrs. Romanovich? What an interesting name for someone with a zoo family of animals, and how lucky she was to make her living sharing them with others. I immediately pictured Mrs. Romanovich as a red-cheeked grandmother who took care of each creature with her special, loving touch. Perhaps she held the baby piglets in her lap as she gave them their bottles. Maybe she fed the bushy llamas by hand, kissing their woolly heads. And maybe, just maybe, Mrs. R. spoke gently to my Dirt.

For a minute, I felt jealous of those tended to in such a doting, devoted way. The way my mother did when I was just a little kid. I thought of how she used to sit with me at night before I'd fall asleep, grazing my hand with her fingertips.

"Butterfly kisses," she'd murmur. "These are butterfly kisses of the fingertips."

But then I snapped back to reality and remembered what Itty had said about Carlo. There wouldn't be any piglets and baby bottles. There wouldn't be any butterfly kisses.

I turned back to the flyer and studied the picture of the ferocious tiger again. I hoped that Mrs. R. and Itty Bitty's brother had kept Dirt safely away from all the other animals in the zoo.

In any case, tiger or not, I was definitely on the right track to find my pony, who had seemed so far, but now was near.

My hands began to shake and I felt my face flush. Holding on tightly to the orange flyer, I ran all the way down the long sloped sidewalk until I realized I had absolutely no idea where I was.

Gathering my wits about me and trying to catch my breath, I looked down at the flyer all over again, then up at the green metal street sign right above my head. A boy on a bike flew by at the exact same time, unnerving me so that I tripped and fell splat right on the sidewalk. Not a pretty sight. And to add to my shame, an elderly man walking a small, freckled spaniel stopped across the street to stare as I gingerly checked out my leg.

"You okay, kid?" he called. And before I knew what was what, he and his pooch dashed toward me. A bit forward, to my mind. "Hurt yourself?"

I shook my head. I certainly didn't need or want any help from anyone. I was on a mission that couldn't be delayed—there wasn't a single second to spare. The dog nibbled at my ankle as if it were a biscuit, and the man gently helped me to my feet. Again, a bit forward for my taste. I could stand up on my own and had always done so, thank you very much.

"Nasty fall. You sure you're all right?"

The man was wearing a dark knit cap and a leather jacket. He spoke slowly, as if wrestling with each and every word. For a second, I thought of Mr. Prattle, the quiet Pa.

I nodded again and tried to smile in an attempt to be convincing, then leaned down to rub the top of the pup's shiny head. He spun around in excitement, then jumped up on two legs. And before I knew what was happening, the freckled spaniel started to hump my very own left calf.

Humping is just a sign of an animal wanting to take charge, show dominance. Well, that pup could most certainly forget that. No dog—or human, for that matter—was about to dominate me.

The man laughed nervously, clearly embarrassed, although I didn't know why. Animals were just like humans, creatures of habit, instinct, and need. In order to demonstrate that I wasn't offended, I leaned down to pet the dog again. The orange flyer flew out of my hand, immediately picked up by a sudden breeze. I lunged to catch it but the pup was ahead of me, leaping high in the air and snapping up the paper in his mouth.

"Good boy!" the old man said proudly, dislodging it from a set of miniature teeth. "I've trained him to catch Frisbees. Guess he thought your paper was one."

I took the flyer back with a sigh of relief, then pointed to the address printed under the tiger's mean face. Maybe this man could direct me.

"Are you sure you're okay?" The man was ignoring my pointed finger and studying my face instead. "Are you sure you're okay and don't need any help?"

I was not okay. I did need help. And he could give it by showing me the way to South Stammer Road. Somehow, some way, I needed to let this man know what I needed and wanted.

I surprised myself by grabbing the man's hand and then pointing to the street sign just above. He looked confused. I shook the flyer in front of his face and underlined "South Stammer Road" with an invisible line, using my index finger like a pen.

I had to make him pay attention. I couldn't just wait around anymore. Now was the time to speak without saying a word.

"Oh!" The man looked relieved. "No problem, you aren't far at all. I can most definitely help you with that! I used to have a good friend who lived on the very next street."

And then, finally, to my enormous relief, the old man with the dog gave me directions all the way to where I needed to go.

It didn't take me long to find my way across the Holler Hollow town square, under the overpass, three more blocks all the way past the bottom of the hill, where Converse Street trailed to a dead end. I stood there for a moment in front of a low brick building that reminded me of a prison and noticed a bitter stench so raw and foul that it almost stopped me dead in my tracks. The odor was coming from across the narrow street, where a large tin sign was posted on a tree.

The sign was so big that I could read it from where I was standing. It had a long black arrow that hung downward, as if pointing below toward you-know-where, although I could see that one side had simply been dislodged from its fastener, bumping ominously against the tree in the wind.

I was nervous. I was excited. I was scared.

I didn't know what to expect; I was dizzy with the rotten air swirling around my face. But I knew exactly what the sign would say before I even read it. And so it did, printed in crimson, the very same color of blood:

MRS. ROMANOVICH'S EXOTIC PETTING ZOO.

And below in smaller lettering: NO FOOD OR DOGS ALLOWED. NO PUBLIC BATHROOMS. NO REFUNDS. NO EXCEPTIONS. ENTER AT YOUR OWN RISK.

Of course, that was my exact plan. I would enter at my own risk in order to rescue Dirt and bring him home.

Mrs. Romanovich's Exotic Petting Zoo

I can tell you this—I was nervous as all get-out standing there smack in front of the sign to the zoo. But I was excited too, just thinking that my Dirt might be a few steps away. It had been so long since I'd seen him or buried my face in his mane, his warm pony neck; the thought of it was thrilling, and I felt goose bumps on both arms. And my plan to rescue him made my heart race. I knew he must be frightened and wondering where I was. How had I let this happen, been so careless that the authorities had to stick in their noses and I had to scare Dirt away?

Nothing would stop me now.

That is, if Itty Bitty's brother hadn't sold my pony all over again.

The stench was sickening. Now more like the smell of

manure, urine, and rot. I was starting to wonder about Mrs. Romanovich and worry for my pony.

I walked ahead slowly through the ghastly air, trembling at the thought of getting closer and closer to Dirt. And when I followed the uneven dirt path that was lined by wide trees, I finally saw a small cabin and plywood lean-to of some kind. I closed my eyes and opened them again, then continued forward. There, on one side of the cabin, was a gigantic wire enclosure.

The wind picked up and I pulled my parka tightly against my chest.

There wasn't a sign of anyone or anything, hide nor hair. I walked right up to the large wire pen, but it was completely empty; then I jiggled the tarnished gate, but it refused to open, so I kicked it out of pure frustration.

"What the heck!" A loud voice rumbled from inside the shack and then a short, fat man appeared, his belly quivering in a white undershirt. He wasn't as large as Itty Bitty and had a much deeper voice. I figured he still could be the brother, but couldn't be sure. He glared at me, then growled like a dog. "What the heck are you doing here, kid? Leave my fence alone. Can't you see that we're closed and that the animals are put away? No one allowed on the property. No viewing of animals or anything else. No zoo. In fact, you're trespassing."

"Who is it, Carlo?" I heard a woman call. Then I knew the man was really Itty Bitty's brother, since Itty had mentioned his name when I visited him in his tiny trailer. And the female voice? Could it be Mrs. Romanovich herself?

Carlo stomped away as quickly as he came, slamming the shack door behind him. "No one," he yelled back. "It's no one at all. Just go back to doing what you do best, Jolene—looking pretty."

I couldn't help but think it rude for Carlo to tell the woman to shut up and wondered if Jolene was Mrs. Romanovich in the flesh, although the two names didn't really seem to fit. But perhaps Jolene might have been kinder and willing to share more information than Itty's horrid brother. And Carlo calling me "no one" really made me mad.

In any case, I would stand my ground, one way or another.

Since the animal pen was made of wire, I could see all the way inside, and there wasn't any question that critters had been kept there recently. Scattered pellets and rotting lettuce were still left out in the open, along with a bale of hay, a trough of greenish water, and blackened turds of every shape, large and small. But there was a particular mound that made my heart skip a beat. I recognized it as similar to those in my very own bedroom of the little crooked house where I used to clean up my pony's smelly mess night and day.

Here was some evidence that Dirt might have been there

earlier, although, of course, I realized it might have been left by a different animal instead.

It made me sad to see how badly the zoo animals had been taken care of. A few lopsided crates marked PIGS lay sideways on a pile of gravel, and a small square of the enclosure was roped off for BABY GOATS and DONKEYS. Hardly enough room for one goat, and it was upsetting to think that donkeys might have been crammed inside there too.

A rusted, padlocked cage for the TALKING PIGEON and a tin pail of water rimmed with green algae banged against each other in the breeze.

I saw trash: paper cups, candy-bar wrappers, Styrofoam plates, and plastic bags thrashing together against the wire railing.

The wind was picking up. The trash swirled, then scattered.

So Dirt had been kept here, in this filthy pen.

My heart sank at the thought of him far away from me in this miserable place.

The real question, however, was where had Dirt been taken and where were all the other petting zoo animals? All sold? I looked around for a stable or trailer of some kind, but there was nothing.

I stood there for quite some time, thinking about how lonely and frightened Dirt must have been and probably still was. The afternoon dimmed around me, settling mournfully in the empty pen like the shadow of an animal headed for slaughter.

The shack door flew open again, and this time the man stuck out his head. Then he stomped out the front door, yelling at the top of his lungs. "This here's a warning. Off my property and stop snooping around. I told you we're closed and moving on. Now git."

I saw a dark rifle crossed over his chest.

"Git!" he repeated. "Do you hear me? Scram."

I was frightened then. I stumbled backward and tried not to fall. A rifle was no laughing matter. But I somehow didn't want the man to see how much he'd scared me, so I just turned around slowly and walked back down the dirt path, cool and collected as a cucumber.

It was late afternoon by then and the falling light flickered behind the trees that lined the dirt path, casting a funny color, goldish pink, and then everything went all squiggly. Hungry, as usual, I dug into my pocket for the last two Nabisco cheese-sandwich crackers and looked for a spot to sit down and think. There was a little patch of grass a bit off the path up ahead, so I took a small detour and went for a quick rest and a quick pee behind the bushes.

A sweet fragrance flooded over me as I walked off course, and I was rewarded by a thicket of trees filled with pine needles and moss. Such a relief to have that terrible stench masked. I sank down into the soft ground to consider my next move. Then I heard the oddest sound, like a child or baby in pain, the low moan of some kind of creature in distress. I sat up quickly, looking all around, and then headed straight into the thicket where the sound was coming from.

It got darker and darker as I walked into the deep, and my heart was beating in my chest faster and faster. I heard the moan again, then a thump and a scratching sound. I didn't know whether to keep moving forward or run the other way.

But forward I went, trying to avoid sharp branches in my face and stumbling over rocks and fallen logs. And then finally, the trickle of water, the rinse of sound.

I came upon a small clearing where two very skinny, brownish goats stared up at me, then tried to scamper away, one limping badly and the other barely holding his little head up. I blinked to make sure that my mind hadn't turned soft, but the goats moaned again so I knew they were real. They had managed to move a foot or two ahead and were shaking together by a small creek, taking turns drinking and then bleating one by one. They both startled when they saw me move toward them again.

I crouched down, offering an open hand in the hope that they could see I was someone to be trusted, someone gentle and kind. Then another sound, higher but weak, and I almost fell right over a small creature covered in black. When it squealed, I realized that I had come upon a mud-splattered pig.

An enormous peacock staggered out from the trees to my

right, one glowing wing bent, and its beak dotted with dried blood. I had never seen a peacock before and my heart was in my mouth as I stared at its beauty and distress.

It was clear that these animals were abandoned and that Carlo had probably had something to do with it. Why else would such a collection of creatures be found so close to his house and the petting zoo?

Two brown rabbits stumbled suddenly right across my path, next a small guinea pig or ferret, peeking up from a hole. But where was Dirt? I wanted to stop and help all of them, bring them to safety, one by one, but knew I had to keep pushing myself forward, faster and faster, out of the clearing through the overgrowth, the bushes and vines.

Imagine a place so dark that it almost didn't exist. Think of your worst fears and nightmares, because that's exactly where I was. I struggled ahead in the deep forest, branches scraping my face, tripped over a fallen log, then a stone, and felt a sharp pain in my leg, but continued without breathing, without allowing myself to even think.

An owl hooted, once then twice. Then the howl of something unfamiliar, maybe a coyote ready to pounce. My pants hems were soaking, I had a bloody lip, my parka was torn, and my heart was in my mouth.

And then, from a distance, I saw an enormous shape ahead. It wasn't moving or making a sound, so I crept forward carefully, not sure what it was. Each step brought me closer and yet I still couldn't make it out. The only animal that large would be an elephant or maybe a huge lion of some kind—the tiger picture on the orange zoo flyer flashed in my mind. Holding still for a second, I tried to see what couldn't possibly be there.

I squinted, blinked, and took another step ahead. The shape was frozen, not breathing.

As my eyes adjusted, I saw, to my surprise, that it wasn't an animal at all but some kind of tall car: a trailer or truck.

It was long and white, halfway covered with broken evergreen branches, as if to be disguised. Actually, the truck looked to be more like a van than anything else, the windowless type driven by kidnappers of the worst kind.

I sidled up to it carefully, not wanting to alert Carlo, if he was near, and when I was just a few inches away, I leaned to press my ear to the metal siding. No sounds came from within, not a single bray or neigh, no sign of Dirt or of anything else. But as I almost turned to leave, out of the corner of my eye, I saw the trailer sway, just slightly, and then again.

Something alive was moving inside.

Lost and Found

If you've ever been truly frightened, you know how it feels. A ribbon of sweat runs down your back and all oxygen evaporates, making it impossible to breathe. I stood there by the van, too terrified to move. What if Itty Bitty's brother caught me spying? What would he do?

I didn't know what was in the van right in front of me. The petting zoo flyer showcased a tiger, but was it really possible to keep a wild animal like that in a petting zoo?

Gathering up my courage and recovering my breath, I listened carefully again for any sound from inside. I might have heard a faint rustle, and then a distinct baaing that must have come from a sheep. No roaring tiger and no sounds at all indicating Dirt, but I had to be sure.

The van's door was padlocked shut. The steel lock was hanging from a chain securing the back door, but it wouldn't budge when I tried to pry it open. The van rocked again, this time with more force. And suddenly I heard what I'd been waiting for for so long.

A soft whinny, a blustery bray, a stomping of impatient hooves. Was it my imagination, too good to be true? And just as I was about to jump up and down with pure joy, I heard a man's gruff voice.

"I told you, Jolene, we gotta get all packed up and ready and be out of here first thing, so pick it up, why don't you."

I swallowed hard and scooted behind a thick-trunked tree, then backed up slowly to another one and crouched down low all over again. The bottom branches were covering me but I could still see all the way through. This time, my worst fears were coming true: Itty Bitty's brother was walking quickly right up to the white van with some woman at his side. Mrs. R.?

The woman hobbled next to Carlo in impossibly high shoes, and her platinum hair was teased to the high heavens, reminding me of a cotton-candy treat.

"Hurry up, woman." Itty's brother was clearly annoyed, and I saw his companion stop to adjust her tight jeans that looked painted on. I couldn't see their faces, only the backs of their heads.

"If we're not there by four a.m., there's no deal." Carlo was tugging on one of her arms. To my horror, I could see a large hunting knife laced to his belt. It glinted in the afternoon sun as if alive. "The boss man up there is meeting us with the cash and is willing to buy the whole lot without any health records. But it's got to happen before dawn, so get a move on."

Who was the boss man? Who was Carlo selling all the animals to? Then the woman trotted to catch up and when she got close, I saw that they were both carrying cardboard boxes of some kind. Probably, hopefully, some kind of feed.

Carlo tugged at the padlock and turned it with a tiny key.

I heard a familiar whinny, then a nicker, then a full-blown neigh. It took every ounce of self-control not to fly to my pony's side, right then and there. I couldn't see much when they entered the van. I did hear clearly, however, the woman's high-pitched squeal: "Oh, Carlo. This is disgusting. I can't stand the smell. And all this poop is gross, gonna ruin my new shoes. And what's the point, anyway, of bothering to feed them now? What difference does it make if they won't be alive for long?"

"For God's sake, Jolene, do I have to go over it all again? Can't you keep one thought in your stupid head? The factory won't buy anything in bad shape, any animal that's sick or dead. Is this really so difficult to understand? Who cares, anyway. Just do what you're told so we're ready to get out of town right after the meet-up."

I thought I might faint right then and there.

They were in and out of the van in a few minutes. I watched as Jolene stumbled out the back door. Her cotton-candy hair was a mess and there were two huge brown stains on her knees. Carlo followed, swearing under his breath. He locked up and they both headed back the way they came, the boxes left behind.

"Darn," Carlo yelled, suddenly stopping midstep, to my horror and dismay. I'd hoped that they'd gone for good and I'd never see either of them again. "I forgot to attach the hitch."

"Carlo! You promised me this would only take a few minutes." The woman had stopped to rub her feet.

Itty's brother looked at her with disgust, then shook his head slowly. "Never mind, I don't have the patience right now anyway. I'll deal with the hitch later."

"I still don't know why we had to feed them tonight, anyway. It's not like one night is going to make a difference," Jolene whined as they started out again.

"Shut it!" Carlo was already walking again. "Didn't I just say not another word? Hurry up and don't be complaining about every single little thing. You don't want me to show you what for, do you? Because one more word and I will."

Jolene followed him silently until they both disappeared.

I knew they still might return again at any time. I couldn't afford to relax for one second, so I ran to the van and jiggled the padlock once, then twice. But it remained stubbornly closed, no key in sight. I banged on the door in frustration, then remembered who was inside. The last thing I wanted to do was frighten him, or any other animal, for that matter.

Dirt. I pressed my lips against the crack in the van's back door. *Dirt, I'm right here, outside, and I'm going to rescue you. I promise. I'll figure out something. Cross my very own heart. I'll get you out of there.*

While the padlock still loomed as a challenge, I had a few good ideas. My father's friend's lock-picking instructions could certainly come in handy now. So I searched my pockets for a safety pin or something else that might work, but there wasn't anything useful to be found, nothing at all. My next idea was bolder, something I had never tried. What if I banged the padlock open with my own brute strength? But I'd have to find some kind of tool, something heavy and sharp.

I flashed on what Carlo had said to Jolene right before they started back home. Something about a hitch for a trailer that he left behind, and I knew that car hitches were made of iron, the perfect instrument for my plan. So just maybe I could pound the padlock open with the hitch that Carlo had left by the van.

I found the hitch leaning on one of the van's back tires. But when I tried to pull the darn thing up in the air so I could use it to smash open the padlock, I figured that I was in big trouble. There was no possible way. The hitch was huge and wouldn't budge, despite my considerable strength. So I picked up a rock that was shaped like a fist and smashed it down on the padlock as hard as possible.

The noise echoed loud as a rifle shot. I knew the noise might draw Carlo back, but I had to risk it. No choice. I hammered away like there was no tomorrow.

The padlock swung under the force, but it didn't splinter the way I'd hoped—for a frantic second I couldn't figure out the next step. And just as I was about to sink to my knees, I saw the van's back door start to wobble off of its hinge. Encouraged, I ran back a few steps, then leapt ahead at full tilt, kicking at the door with my foot. It jiggled, then fell open at the corner, just an inch or so, but when I kicked it again, lo and behold.

The door fell, almost all the way to the ground, and I waited, trembling, for the imprisoned animals to jump out, along with my Dirt. But the opposite happened, to my surprise. There wasn't a single sound or a movement of any kind.

So slowly, holding my breath, I craned my neck and looked inside.

I was shocked by what I found.

The tiniest lamb cowering by his mother, both of them covered with hay and grime. I shivered, but still I didn't stop climbing up into the van. Holding back my tears, I stepped around the poor animals and forward into the dim. And at the far end of the van, I heard that familiar sound. My pony was crying out for me; he knew I was there.

I lunged toward his voice, tripping and falling on the van's floor. Something soft nibbled at my ankle, and despite myself, I shooed it away. My only goal was to get through the dark, all the way to my Dirt.

I was weeping then, my face swimming with tears. I

lunged again, aching to call out my pony's name. I could hear his whine.

Something raised its head in a wire crate. It growled and then dropped back down. I held on to one wall and inched myself around a black dog or large cat. It lay on one side, panting.

I wanted to stop. Walking by seemed heartless. But for now, there was only one.

Dirt was standing still as a statue when I finally reached him at the van's far corner, his head bowed low to the floor. It was too dark to see his one eye, but I imagined its sorrowful glance. I walked toward my pony carefully at first, then threw both my arms around his damp, limp neck.

Dirt was tied to a metal hook with a thick braided rope. I could see that his mane was knotted, his fur raw on his flank where he sometimes rubbed when nervous. It had only been four days since I'd driven him away, but he somehow looked as if it had been weeks. Animals need to be loved the same as humans do, and I understood that Dirt was hungry for more than just food. As I ran my hand over his body, we both shuddered.

I managed to untie the rope from the hook, but couldn't seem to loosen the piece around his neck. It didn't really matter, anyway. Dirt was free now and he was coming with me.

J. Herriot, DVM

And so we both left the van together slowly and, sadly, left the other animals as well. Dirt stumbled twice but followed my lead, and I stroked his muzzle, his ears, and his mangled mane as we walked. I kissed him on his downy mouth, and his warm breath on my face gave me confidence that he was okay.

But then the wound. It started at his knee and slithered all the way up to his shoulder, as if someone had sliced him open with a knife. A buzz of black flies circled, and yellow pus rimmed its jagged edge.

I never sobbed as hard as I did then, heaving in gulps and gasps. I sobbed because Dirt was hurt. I sobbed because I had frightened him away with the green hose on that terrible day. Because we had been lost to each other and because I had been lost to myself for so long.

I knew I had to find help, quickly get my pony medicine, food, and drink, but he was so weak that I hated to make him hurry. As I struggled to figure out what I should do next, I remembered the shop next the Holler Hollow hardware store where I'd been earlier that day.

It seemed weeks had passed since I had stopped at the mini-mart for crackers and Coke; strange that it had only been a few hours ago when I found the flyer for the horrid petting zoo. Paws and Claws, wasn't that the name of the shop right next door to the hardware store bulletin board? With a name like that, the place had to have something to do with animals, there was no doubt. Maybe it was a pet store of some kind that sold medicine and such. Of course, I knew it was getting late and the place might be closed, but you never knew. And I could always break in if I had to. I would do anything to help Dirt.

I continued walking ahead, then motioned to Dirt to pick up his speed. While I hated to rush him, I worried that Carlo might find us if we didn't make it to town soon and that the wound would worsen. Dirt struggled to obey, then stumbled again. He was a hurt and exhausted Shetland pony whose life was in my hands. And I finally realized that even I couldn't save Dirt all by myself. I could do many things for my pony, including keeping him from being sold for horse-meat and rescuing him from Carlo, but I couldn't heal all that needed healing.

Still, Dirt somehow managed to regain his footing, to

obey my command, but then suddenly stopped in his tracks. When I touched the rope still hanging around his neck, he rested his head on my shoulder while we waited together for him to regain his strength. And then we continued on all over again, side by side, both of us uncertain if we would make it all the way out of the dark woods.

It must have taken us close to an hour just to cover the short dirt path all the way to the end, turn right at the bottom of the hill, and struggle three more blocks under the overpass, where we had to stop for another rest. Dirt was sweating then, his spotty coat moist and warm. I rubbed my pony's soft nose with one finger—still velvet, still scattered with silky whiskers. He quivered, then put his bedraggled ear to my mouth as if to listen for silent instructions.

Not far, my boy, not too much farther to go.

I kept looking back quickly, just to make sure Carlo wasn't following behind. It was terrifying to think that he might suddenly appear. What if he'd noticed that the van had been broken into and that Dirt was gone? What if he followed us?

It was dark, and not a single person was outside. Even the stores were closed. I shivered, but I couldn't panic. I had to hold my ground.

Paws and Claws was there just as I remembered, a small,

peeling clapboard house, probably closed for the day. Still, I motioned for Dirt to stay and walked up the porch steps to knock on the front door.

No answer for a moment, and then I heard a rustle, then footsteps, then a "Who in the high heavens!" and the door was flung open wide.

The woman was wearing a dingy blue work shirt, blue jeans, and gray slippers worn down at the toes. Her thick white hair was caught in two braids, and her eyes snapped fiercely behind rimless glasses. "What on earth?"

I blinked at her, lower lip trembling, and she blinked right back at me.

Her name was Jane Herriot, DVM, and she was a doctor of veterinary medicine. At first, she told me that she'd have to contact my parents right away and that she was alarmed that I was out all alone at night and that I wouldn't say a word. But then she saw Dirt behind me, trying to hobble up the front steps, and she flew into overdrive.

Dr. Jane cleaned Dirt's wound with ointment brought outside from her office and spoke to him in a quiet, gentle tone. Then she took my arm with an iron grip and pulled me out of Dirt's line of vision, as if not to upset him.

"Don't be a ninny," Dr. Jane hissed. "If you don't tell me how to contact your parents, I'll have to call the sheriff right away. Now spit it out, rug rat. Oh, I forgot you don't speak."

Dr. Jane wasn't very good at hiding her irritation.

Dirt was a sick pony, Dr. Jane, DVM, told me, his wound already infected. He needed to be boarded and supervised. Did I understand this, the gravity of the situation? Was this pony mine? How did he end up in such bad condition? At this, she shot me a sharp, suspicious look. Where did I live? Did my parents know where I was, out all alone at night? What had happened? Who was to blame?

She peppered me with questions, but of course, I remained mum, nodding or shaking my head when appropriate. DVM wasn't a particularly patient doctor, finally slamming down her fist, something that must have hurt quite a bit.

"Here's what we're going to do. Listen up, because I never mince my words." She stood up and faced me, straightening her shoulders as if entering a boxing ring. "Unless you tell me who your parents are and what happened to this poor creature, I'll immediately call the police. This pony's been mistreated, and children don't usually knock on strangers' doors all by themselves. And looks like I'm not going to get an answer from you."

I looked right into DVM's face and understood right then and there that she was two people: Dr. Jane and DVM. Dr. Jane was much nicer. You wouldn't want to mess with DVM.

"Well?" Her hands were on her hips. It was clear she meant business.

How could I respond when I didn't speak? How could I let her know where I'd come from, what I'd been through, what I'd seen? I had to make her understand. All at once, my mother, my father, Heywood Prune, the authorities, foster care, the dying animals, my lost pony in terrible pain, crashed down over my head. I opened my mouth and put my hand on my chest. It was hurting so much that my teeth chattered.

Silence had always protected me from falling apart, from keeping the past from storming loudly back to life.

And yet Dirt was sick and needed good care. I would do anything to help him, no doubt about that. So I sidled up close to my pony, my back to DVM, and nuzzled his face the way he always nuzzled me. Then I spun around again and motioned with one hand, indicating that I needed paper and a pen.

I would give DVM the information she needed. There wasn't just one way to communicate the truth, after all.

I wrote down the Prattles' names and the phone number that Mrs. Prattle had written down for me on my first morning of foster care. I shared this with Dr. Jane, not because I wanted the Prattles to pick me up but because Dirt needed treatment.

"I'll contact them immediately, but your pony will have to stay here for two weeks or so and then we'll see. I'll board him with the other large animals in my barn near the house.

Someone's always there, even when I'm at work. That way we can make sure that he gets the necessary care."

I nodded. If Dirt needed to board with Dr. Jane, then his health had to come first. I had thought that bunking in the little crooked house with Dirt was best for both of us. I had been wrong. Defeat washed over me, almost buckling my knees. There was no bringing Dirt back to the little crooked house now.

Dr. Jane tied Dirt to her porch post with the loose piece of rope still around his neck, and ushered me inside. She sat us down together in her cramped living room, me in a tan leather armchair. It was clear that she meant business. "I need to know why this animal's been mistreated and who's responsible."

I motioned for the paper and pen again, and next to the Prattles' names and address, wrote:

Mrs. R.'s Exotic Petting Zoo.

When Dr. Jane read my words, I thought she might split a gut. Her face flushed red and she took off her glasses and rubbed her eyes.

She told me that Carlo was a known criminal. He had been in trouble with the law several times before, but the petting zoo scheme was something new this fall. She'd found out about it from the flyer on the bulletin board next door and sent in a complaint to the local Humane Society. Dr. Jane thought it was possible there was a warrant out on him. It was no wonder that he was trying to sneak out of town.

I nodded. I had to make Dr. Jane understand. It wasn't just the zoo that was the problem. It was Carlo and his evil factory plan.

I grabbed the paper I'd just written on and jotted down more:

Animals will be sold to a factory at four a.m.

"Four a.m.? Why that early?" Dr. Jane looked confused, and then her expression turned to thunder. "By law, any factories making use of animals must have documentation, health histories to ensure there aren't any transmittable viruses or the like. After all, body parts can be dangerous if infected."

I must have gasped, because Dr. Jane's voice immediately softened. "It's okay, rug rat. That's not going to happen. You've done something good here. Believe me, I'll be on the phone to the sheriff shortly."

But what about the others? The animals that weren't healthy enough to sell?

"Something else on your mind, rug rat?" Dr. Jane was studying my face carefully. She looked confused.

I opened my arms wide to indicate that I needed more from her, more of her attention, more of her care, more help. I needed for her to find all the animals and give them refuge.

Dr. Jane just patted my head quickly and took out her phone. I could see that she was about to call the sheriff as promised.

First, I'd have to tell her about all the others.

I grabbed one of Dr. Jane's hands and placed it on my chest. My heart was cantering so hard that I was out of breath. Again, she looked confused. "Feeling okay, rug rat?"

I was not okay.

I had to do something to make her understand and act.

I reached for the pen and paper. I would write everything that was still alive in my heart.

I had the sudden memory of my mother handing me her pink childhood seashell and telling me to listen.

"You'll hear a muffled song," she'd said. "It's a family of mermaids calling each other home."

All these years later, I heard the shell's echo as I wrote down eight important words in the darkest, boldest print possible:

There are other animals to be rescued too.

Recovery

I must have conked out in Dr. Jane's armchair for a bit, because I had the strangest dream. Something about the Shetland Islands so far away. Something about a turquoise ocean and a bridge to a peaceful, united kingdom.

When I woke up, Dr. Jane was sitting by my side.

"The Prattles are on the way," she said to me, taking my hands in hers. "It won't be much longer now."

I rubbed my eyes. Then I remembered where I was and why.

"I want you to know," Dr. Jane continued, "that animal control is out there now, collecting all the mistreated and abandoned critters. And Carlo is in custody." She looked at me steadily. "You've done more than most adults would have."

I looked away. I was going to be leaving Dirt soon.

He'd be taken care of and would get better, but the two of us would never live together again the way we'd done before.

When the horse trailer came to pick up my pony in front of Paws and Claws, Dirt turned to look at me.

He shook his beautiful shaggy head and blinked his one eye.

I inhaled his raw, salty-sweet scent—the fuel needed for me to carry on.

There was a burning in my throat, and I wiped my eyes with both hands as Dirt was driven away.

It couldn't have been more than thirty minutes later when the Prattles arrived.

Mrs. Prattle, never an example of calm, arrived at Dr. Jane's house wailing and pressing her hand to her heart. She hugged me so tightly for so long that I thought I just might choke. Then, weeping and making a horrible scene, she hugged me all over again, talking a mile a minute to Dr. Jane. My shirt was sopping wet from Prattle tears.

Dr. Jane might have rolled her eyes at me in sympathy over one shoulder, but I couldn't be quite sure. I wasn't used to having someone see things the way I did.

Finally collecting herself, Mrs. Prattle told me that my father was doing well and had already started talking. He was being cared for in a rehabilitation home just outside of Shelter. I could visit him soon, once I got some rest.

"But he's been very worried about you, Yonder, dear." Mrs. Prattle frowned, underscoring her point. "The stress of not knowing where you were didn't do him much good when he was trying to heal."

"Didn't you just say that her father was doing well?" Dr. Jane asked sharply. "Let's give the kid a break."

"Well, I suppose so." Mrs. Prattle looked flustered.

Pa was waiting in the car and got out quickly when he saw me. He took my right hand in his and then kissed it as if I was a princess of some kind. Then, holding his fedora close to his chest, he bowed.

"You are a wonder, Miss Yonder," he said softly. "I hear you found what you were looking for all by yourself."

"Hurry along, now, you two," Mrs. Prattle called, scurrying to the car with Dr. Jane right behind. "Dr. Herriot has been very kind, but it's getting late. Let's get on our way so that both she and Yonder can get some rest."

And just as Pa was helping me settle myself in the car, Dr. Jane called out:

"Wait. With all the commotion, we didn't cement our plans. When can Yonder come back to participate in her pony's care? I think it important that she be involved in the process of healing." Dr. Jane stood there in the chilly night, arms crossed over her chest and squinting through her lopsided glasses. "Let's get the terms settled so we're all in clear agreement before you all go off on your way."

DVM was making a reappearance, lock, stock, and barrel. My heart leapt right out of my chest in relief, and I thought of handing it right over to Dr. Jane in an offering of gratitude and friendship.

"Oh," Mrs. Prattle said, busying herself by knotting an itchy woolen scarf tightly around my neck. "Oh no, Yonder most certainly can't come back here again. Why, she'll have schoolwork to attend to and quite a bit of catching up to do. But I appreciate you taking care of that pony, who's been such trouble for our girl."

There was dead silence then. Not that Mrs. Prattle noticed.

I squeezed my hands into two tight fists until my fingernails cut my palms. Didn't Prattle realize that I wasn't just a kid who didn't speak, but a person who knew her own mind? That I could be responsible for what I owed?

I shook my head so vigorously that I made myself dizzy. I would help care for Dirt, no matter what anyone said.

DVM took off her glasses and gripped them tightly with one fist. I noticed her right foot tap, tap, tapping on the nearly frozen ground. Then I could swear I saw actual steam rising from her ears and mouth.

"Mrs. Prattle," she said through clenched teeth, "I'm not prepared to accept—"

Then, to my amazement, I heard a quiet voice interrupt. It was low and soft, but also firm.

"Yonder has shown us all that she has remarkable courage," Pa said, stepping forward out of the shadows. "Why, if it wasn't for her, that pony would probably be dead. I've read that Shetland ponies are the strongest of all horses—well, I think our Yonder is the strongest of all girls."

"P-pa," Mrs. Prattle sputtered, "I don't think—"

"Not another word," Pa said, taking my arm. "Yonder and the pony will do as the good doctor instructs. She has most certainly earned the right. The issue is settled."

Dr. Jane nodded, Mrs. Prattle looked flustered, and I smiled at Pa as he helped me into the car. I waved to DVM out of the window as we pulled away, and to my complete surprise, good ole Dr. Jane actually blew me a kiss.

You-know-who chattered nonstop all the way back to Shelter, but I didn't even mind. I sank into the backseat, my eyes almost immediately closing, my parka wrapped tightly around me like a cocoon.

The next two days were hazy. I slept. I ate my meals on a tray in bed because Mrs. Prattle insisted that I "get my rest." Strange, because I found myself in the same pink foster bedroom as before I ran away, but this time I didn't feel sad. I was ready to be taken care of for a while and happy that my pony was being tended to at the same time.

I slept more. I ate more. I read a horse magazine that Pa bought for me. I even had a visitor: Trudy Trumpet, but Mrs. Prattle shooed her out of the room so I wouldn't get tired out.

But before Trudy left, I tried to shake her hand. I wanted her to know that I didn't hate her anymore. And as far as social workers went, I figured she really wasn't so bad. After all, there was no one else who reached out to me when I really didn't know that reaching out was what I needed. Except, of course, for Dirt.

Typical of Trudy, she just brushed away my hand, laying a wet smooch on my cheek.

I thought this inappropriate behavior for a social worker, but smiled weakly anyway. I had the feeling that wasn't the last I'd be seeing of Ms. Trudy Trumpet.

Dr. Jane called both afternoons to report on Dirt's progress and let me know how the other rescued animals were doing. Not all of them had made it, but my pony was improving, although still weak and in need of antibiotics. She told me that I was expected to report for work by the next week, unless I had a doctor's note indicating that I was too ill. And that I'd be assigned to mucking out the barn for two hours straight each day. No excuses. DVM wasn't kidding when she told me that she didn't mince words.

On my third day back at the Prattles', I went downstairs for breakfast and waited for Mrs. Prattle to finish making my eggs. A long white envelope, addressed to me in pencil, fluttered on the kitchen table when I sat down.

"It looks like you have some mail, Yonder, dear. Who could it be from? No return address, although it's postmarked Shelter."

But I immediately knew, tearing it open as fast as possible. This is what the letter said:

Dear Yonder,

This is your father writing to you.
I want you to know that I'm getting well
 and I'll be going home soon.
I hope that you will come back home with
me for a new start.
 I'll build your pony a shed out back and
keep him out of the cold.

From Your Father

I read the letter twice, folded it carefully, and put it back on the table. I was happy to hear from my father and also very relieved. But to my surprise, something was nagging at me. It was very kind of my father to offer his help with Dirt and to build him a shed, but I knew in my heart of hearts that it might not happen. I'd learned that there could be more than just one person in your life, and that was okay. I could open the door and make myself known.

"Doggone it," Mrs. Prattle muttered suddenly in a surprisingly grumpy voice. "Why, it's just October and it's beginning to snow already. Guess it's time to get out the old blower, Pa."

I spun around to the window and saw a sprinkling of white. Ignoring Mrs. Prattle's protests, I dashed outside without stopping for my coat and stretched open both arms. The snow was falling sideways, tingeing the ground and trees silver. Tilting my head backward, I laughed, icy flakes melting in my throat.

Somewhere in a red barn stall thirty miles north, Dirt raised his head and listened. He heard my laughter from afar.

Dr. Jane had told me on the phone that wounds can take months to heal all the way deep down. "We can't forget to protect the scab so it doesn't reopen, rug rat," she'd said in her grouchy DVM voice. "Be patient, for goodness' sake. Don't expect the impossible; recovery won't happen overnight."

The snow came down harder but I wasn't cold. I stood still and listened for sounds of lost animals as they wandered through the winter forest and fields. I couldn't rescue them all myself, but I had rescued some.

A cluster of tiny mysteries exploded down over me,

twinkling silvery white. They sparkled for a minute, then disappeared.

I'd always known that words only mattered if they added up to the truth. I might not ever speak out loud, but I'd always have my own voice. And even if I never made another sound, I sure could make some noise.

There was a fork in the rocky road up ahead, and I knew exactly which way to go.

Author's Note

The idea for *Dirt* came to me years ago, when two cheeky and remarkable Shetland ponies named McNeill and Duncan trotted into my life. I was the head of a school for children with learning differences and got a call from a Shetland pony rescue organization. They had a pair of therapy ponies and knew we had a barn. Would we take them?

Our new "pony curriculum" was a hit with the students. They braided manes to improve fine motor skills; they measured the ponies from hoof to haunch for math; they wrote pony stories and drew pony pictures for English and art. For science, the students took their own blood pressure before and after a visit to the barn. It was almost always lower after time with McNeill and Duncan.

McNeill, my personal favorite, was by far the worse behaved. Once, to the great amusement of the students, he pushed me into a pile of manure, and I can't count the times that he looked me straight in the eye and splattered me with mud. But McNeill was particularly patient with the students. However mischievous he was with me, he always welcomed them with a soft nuzzle, standing stock-still to be fussed over and kissed. He seemed to know how much he meant to the kids, and he was the perfect nonjudgmental listener as they practiced reading aloud by whispering in his soft pony ear. Many of our students struggled, and what struck me was the joy and confidence the ponies brought them.

When no one hears what you say or understands the way you think, a fat pony with a gleam in his eye can make all the difference. *Dirt* is a book for any kid who needs a friend, even if it's a four-legged one.

Here are some local and national organizations to contact if you or someone you know needs a therapy animal in their life:

Personal Ponies
www.personalponies.org

Canine Partners for Life, Pennsylvania
www.k94life.org

Bright Spot Therapy Dogs, Massachusetts
www.bright-spot.org

—Denise Gosliner Orenstein

Acknowledgments

I am in great debt to my editor, the extraordinary Rachel Griffiths, who tended to this manuscript with exquisite care and passion. Her enthusiasm, insight, humor, and expert guidance helped me bring Dirt and Yonder home. It has been my great fortune to have an editor so devoted and to whom every word mattered.

A note of great appreciation to Emily Seife and all the dedicated members of *Dirt*'s Scholastic team, including Nina Goffi, Elizabeth Tiffany, Lauren Donovan, Tracy van Straaten, Lizette Serrano, Rachel Feld, Antonio Gonzalez, and Roz Hilden and all the brilliant members of the sales team. Each of you brought something special to the book.

Thank you to Ginger Knowlton, my agent at Curtis Brown, who believed in *Dirt* early on and worked tirelessly on the book's behalf.

And to my remarkable daughters: Lisa, who loved *Dirt* from the get-go, and Jennifer, who one day will read this book to her young son.

I'm also grateful to my dear friend of forty-nine years, Twig Craighead George—fierce and loyal advocate of my work.

To Margaret Leardi, who brought us Duncan and McNeill, and who cared for them with devotion.

Lee Trainer, your support of the animals made a difference for the students, and your cranky wisdom made a difference for me. Thank you.

Always to my sister, Kathy Gosliner, steadfast and true.

Ann Marie and Katie, thank you for rescuing me that dark night in the barn. Your light shines a long and wondrous path.

About the Author

Denise Gosliner Orenstein has taught at American University in Washington, DC, as well as in bush villages throughout the state of Alaska. She has also cooked for an Alaskan village prison, worked as a PEN prison writing mentor, and taught literature classes and assisted in a canine therapy program for inmates. Most recently, as head of a school for children with learning differences, she introduced a curriculum based on two rescued Shetland ponies. Denise is the mother of two daughters and lives in Northampton, Massachusetts.